U0088074

最多人使用的

關鍵

英語 學習法

國家圖書館出版品預行編目資料

最多人使用的英語關鍵學習法 / 潘威廉著
-- 初版. -- 新北市：雅典文化，民105.07
　　面；　公分. -- (全民學英文；39)
ISBN 978-986-5753-67-2(平裝附光碟片)

　　1. 英語　　　2. 學習方法
805.1　　　　　　　　　　105007653

全民學英文系列　39

最多人使用的英語關鍵學習法

著／潘威廉
責任編輯／潘紹杰
美術編輯／王國卿
封面設計／姚恩涵

法律顧問：方圓法律事務所／涂成樞律師

總經銷：永續圖書有限公司　　　CVS代理／美璟文化有限公司
永續圖書線上購物網　　　　　　TEL：(02) 2723-9968
www.foreverbooks.com.tw　　　FAX：(02) 2723-9668

出版日／2016年07月

ⓐ雅典文化

出版社　22103　新北市汐止區大同路三段194號9樓之1
　　　　TEL　(02) 8647-3663
　　　　FAX　(02) 8647-3660

前言

　　有人說到了美國不會開車就像沒有腳一樣，在現今這個地球村的時代，出了國門不會說英語就像沒有嘴巴一樣。作為當今主要國際性語言，英語的重要性是無庸置疑的。

　　然而英語的世界就如同茫茫大海一樣，常讓人覺得有背不完的單字與片語、學不完的文法與句型，對於非英語系國家出生的人而言，想說一口好的英語又談何容易？

　　作者在從事教育工作多年後，逐漸領悟到駕馭英語最直接有效的方式，就是反覆練習最關鍵的英語單字、片語、文法與句型。所謂"最關鍵"指的就是最常出現、最多人使用、以及最簡單易學。

　　在使用最關鍵學習法後，您的說與寫能力將會快速大幅提升，在建立起自信心後，未來再繼續學習如何讓自己的英語能力更加完備。就如同樹根茁壯以後，就不必擔心以後是否能枝葉茂盛。

　　一般而言聽比說容易，讀比寫容易。在您對於說與寫的能力充滿自信心後，聽和讀的能力更不成問題。相信讀者只要跟著本書附贈的mp3 不斷練習，英語能力必能意想不到地突飛猛進。

　　本書與坊間其他書籍最大差異尚包括本書涵蓋生活中每一層面的用語，而非僅侷限於旅遊或飲食等。因此認真讀完本書後將讓讀者的英文程度有全方位的躍進。再者除了正式英語外，本書也涵蓋一般日常生活中常見的口語、俚語、俗語，使讀者能使用與了解更道地、生活化的美語。

　　資訊科技早已融入每個人的生活中，本書的另一特色就是將最關鍵、必學的科技用語納入，讓每一讀者的英語能力不與現代世界脫節。

Chapter 1

問候與社交

.... ● Greetings & Social Interaction

Chapter 2

個人資料

PersonalInformation

Chapter 3

人際關係

Relationships

Chapter 4
傳遞訊息

● Messages

Chapter 5

飲食

●— FoodandDrink

Chapter 6
服裝、鞋子、配件

.... ● Clothing, Shoes, Accessories

Chapter 7
交通

.... ● Transportation

Chapter 8

買賣

● Trade

Chapter 9
工作

• Work

Chapter 10

旅遊休閒

● Travel&Leisure

Chapter 11

健康

● Health

Chapter **1**

問候與社交

Greetings & Social Interaction

面對面問候語基本型

1. Ⓐ How're you doing?
   你好嗎？

   Ⓑ Fine.
   我很好。

2. Ⓐ How's it going?
   你好嗎？

   Ⓑ I am doing well.
   我很好。

3. Ⓐ What's up?
   你好嗎？

   Ⓑ I am doing great.
   我很好。

說明

以上三組問答都是相同的意思，其中What's up? 是較為口語化，一般年輕人較常使用的說法。

4. **A** Hey man, it's good to see you. How are you?

   嗨，哥們，這是很高興見到你。你好嗎？

   B Not too bad.

   不算太壞。

5. **A** Hi Ma'am, you look great today!

   女士，妳今天氣色不錯!

   B Thanks!

   謝謝。

6. **A** Hey dude! What brought you here?

   嘿兄弟，甚麼風把你吹來?

   B Just wanna say hi to you.

   只是想來跟你說聲嗨。

說明

> dude是年輕人對熟人的稱呼。

與對方初次見面時

A My name is Tom. It's a pleasure to know you.
我是湯姆，很高興認識你。

B I'm Tracy, nice to meet you, too.
我是崔西，也很高興見到你。

A My uncle Sam told me a lot about you.
我叔叔山姆告訴我很多關於你的事情。

B He is a really nice guy.
他真是一個好人。

A Hi there, can I join you?
嗨我可以加入你們嗎？

003 **B** Of course!
當然可以！

向人問好

A I haven't seen your mom for 10 years. How is she doing?
我10年沒有看到你媽媽了。她還好嗎？

B She is doing OK except for some eyesight problems
不錯，除了有一些視力問題。

A I miss her so much. She used to hang around with my mom a lot.
我很想念她。她以前與我媽常在一起。

B I remember that. They were close friends.
我記得。他們是親密的朋友。

A Send my best regards to your mom.
向你的母親送上我的問候。

B Thanks. I'll let her know. Say hi to your mom for me.
謝謝。我會讓她知道。替我向你媽媽說嗨。

問候

🅐 Tammy, I haven't seen you for ages.
How are you doing?
譚美，我久沒有看到你了。你怎麼樣？

🅑 I'm doing pretty well. How about you?
我很好。你呢？

🅐 Never better, thanks. How is your kid?
從來沒更好過，謝謝。你的孩子如何？

🅑 Daniel is fine, he's turning 7 years old
this month.
丹尼爾很好，他這個月變7歲了。

🅐 Kids are growing up so fast. I gotta go.
孩子成長如此之快。我得走了。

🅑 See ya.
再見。

尊稱或頭銜

1. Congratulations! Mr. and Mrs. Jones.
   瓊斯先生與瓊斯太太，恭喜！

2. Thank you. Ms. Thompson.
   謝謝妳，湯普森小姐。

3. Ma'am, enjoy your flight.
   女士，請享受妳的航程。

4. Sir, long time no see.
   先生，好久不見。

Sir 與Ma'am後面不加姓名。

5. Thank you, Doctor Hu.
   胡醫師，謝謝你。

攀談

A Do you think I should introduce myself to the manager over there?
你覺得我應該去向那邊的經理自我介紹嗎？

B Why not? If an opportunity comes up, strike up a conversation.
為什麼不呢？如果機會出現，開始和他談話。

A What do I talk about?
該談甚麼？

B Relax. You just try to find out what she's interested in and go with that.
放鬆。試圖找出他的興趣，順著這個話題。

A That easy?
那麼容易？

B Please, you got nothing to lose.
拜託，你又沒有什麼損失。

過年或節日

1. Merry Christmas!
   聖誕快樂！

2. Happy New Year!
   新年快樂！

3. Happy Mother's Day!
   母親節快樂！

4. Happy Mid-Autumn Festival!
   中秋節快樂！

5. Happy Dragon Boat Festival!
   端午節快樂！

6. Happy holidays!
   佳節愉快！

7. Happy Labor Day!
   勞動節快樂！

巧遇朋友

Ⓐ I don't believe this! It's the 2nd time I came across you.
真不敢相信！這是我第二次巧遇你。

Ⓑ Yup, what a surprise!
是的，讓人驚訝！

Ⓐ Do you come to this restaurant often?
你經常來這家餐廳？

Ⓑ I am a regular customer here.
我是這裡的常客。

Ⓐ So how is work going?
工作如何？

Ⓑ Same ole same ole.
老樣子。

說明

same ole same ole 等於 same old same old。

巧遇朋友 2

A What a coincidence!
真是太巧了！

B Yeah, I bump into friends quite often.
是啊，我經常巧遇朋友。

A What have you been up to lately?
你最近做了什麼？

B I just started to work on the new project.
我剛開始從事新專案。

A This is my stop. I'll catch you later.
我要在這個站牌下車。以後再和你聊。

B I'll see you in swimming class, Bye.
游泳課見。

朋友來訪

A Welcome, come on in!
歡迎,進來吧!

B What a nice apartment!
這公寓真不錯!

A How are things with you?
最近怎麼樣呀?

B I am doing pretty well.
我相當好。

A Let me show you around.
讓我帶你四處看看。

B My pleasure.
我喜歡。

A You're an interior designer. Please feel free to give me some advice.
你是一位室內設計師。請隨時給我一些建議。

聚會

A Do you want to join the party tonight? 7 pm at Helen's house.

你想參加今晚的派對嗎？晚上7點在海倫家。

B I wish I could. But I have an exam tomorrow. I am kind of worried about it.

我希望我能。但我明天有一個考試。我有點擔心。

A Alright, In that case, maybe I will see you next time.

好吧，這樣的話，也許下一次。

B Wish me luck!

祝我好運！

A Good luck on your exam! I believe you'll get an A+.

祝你考試好運！我相信你會得到一個A+。

B Thanks! Have fun!

謝謝！玩得開心！

順路拜訪

1. Please drop by when you have time.
   當你有時間時請來坐坐。

2. I will stop by your house on my way home.
   我在回家的路上會順道拜訪你。

 說明

> drop by 和 stop by 都是短暫稍作停留。

3. We're concerned about you. Please drop us a line when you can.
   我們很關心你。如果能，請給我們一個訊息。

4. Drop me a note when you get a chance.
   有機會，請給我一個訊息。

 說明

> drop someone a line 和 drop someone a note 都是給某人打通電話或寫個簡短的電子郵件。

033

等人

A Are you there yet?
你到那裡了沒？

B I'm almost there. Sorry I'm late.
我幾乎快到了。對不起，我遲到了。

A No problem. I just wanted to tell you I'm inside.
沒關係。我只是想告訴你，我在裡面。

B I will be there in 3 minutes.
我會在3分鐘內趕到。

A Take your time.
慢慢來。

B I am wearing a blue scarf.
我圍著一條藍色的圍巾。

介紹

A Sir, have we met before?
先生，我們以前見過面？

B I don't think we've met. I'm Kevin Young.
我不認為我們已經見過面，我是凱文‧楊。

A I am Chris Lin. You must be Bob Young's brother, am I correct?
我是克里斯林。你一定是鮑伯‧楊的弟弟，對嗎？

B That's right! We both resemble our father.
是的！我們兩個都像我們的父親。

A No wonder I thought you look so familiar!
難怪我覺得你看起來這麼眼熟！

B Lots of people mistake me for him.
很多人誤以為我是他。

介紹 2

A Who is the chubby lady standing beside Joe?
站在喬旁邊身材圓潤的女士是誰？

B Oh, that's Michelle, my colleague.
哦，那是密雪兒，我的同事。

A How about the tall guy on her right. What's his name?
她右邊的高個子男生叫什麼名字？

B Her fiancé Doug. He's really good looking, isn't he?
她的未婚夫道格。他長的很好看，不是嗎？

A I wanna know them.
我想認識他們。

B Sure. Let me introduce them to you.
當然。讓我介紹給你。

聯絡感情

Ⓐ Hey Alex, I don't see you around here these days.
嘿亞歷克斯,我這些日子沒在附近看到你。

Ⓑ I moved to downtown several weeks ago.
我幾個星期前搬到市中心。

Ⓐ Keep in touch, pal. Don't be a stranger.
保持聯絡,伙伴。別當陌生人。

Ⓑ Definitely. I'll buzz you every time I come here.
肯定會的。我每次來這裡時會給你電話。

說明

buzz是口語,打電話的意思,例如:give you a buzz---給你電話。
keep in touch等於 stay in touch, 保持聯絡。

稱讚人

1. Your kids are so adorable!
   您的孩子好可愛！

2. Your son is really talented.
   你兒子很有才華。

3. That's very sweet of you.
   你真是讓人窩心。

4. How considerate you are!
   你真體貼！

5. That's very thoughtful of you.
   你考慮很周到。

6. You are such a loving father.
   你真是個慈愛的父親。

7. What a brilliant idea!
   多麼棒的主意！

稱讚人 2

1. What a man of style!
   好一個型男！

2. You are indeed a man of character.
   你確實是有品格的人。

3. Your mom is a lady of great taste.
   你媽媽很有品味。

4. Rosa is a woman of her word.
   羅沙言出必行。

5. Wilson is honorable in word and in deed.
   威爾遜的言行值得尊敬。

6. Ian is one of a kind.
   伊恩是獨一無二的。

7. Rachel is always generous to her friends.
   瑞秋對她的朋友向來慷慨。

安慰祝福人

1. I'm keeping my fingers crossed for you.
   我祝你好運。

2. Everything will work out just fine!
   事情會變好的。

3. Come on! It's not the end of the world.
   拜託！這又不是世界末日。

4. It's darkest right before the dawn.
   黎明前是最黑暗的。

5. The best is yet to come.
   最好的還在後頭。

6. Good things come to those who wait.
   等待的人是有福的。

7. You deserve something better.
   你值得擁有更好的。

安慰祝福人 2

1. Don't make it too hard on yourself.
   不要太苛責自己。

2. He is just a kid. What can you expect?
   他只是個孩子。你還能期望什麼？

3. Life goes on.
   生活得繼續。

4. People make mistakes.
   人非聖賢，孰能無過。

5. There's always a second chance.
   總有第二次機會。

6. Hold on! It's closer than you think.
   堅持！成功比你想的更接近。

7. Don't give up. Your dream will come true.
   不要放棄。你的夢想將要成真。

和外地人交談

A How long have you been here?
妳在這裡多久了？

B Believe it or not. 4 years.
信不信由你。4年。

A No wonder you speak Chinese very well. Is your husband with you?
難怪妳中文說得非常好。妳的丈夫和妳一起嗎？

B Yes, he just got here last month.
是的，他上個月剛來這裡。

A How many times have you been to Hsinchu?
妳去過新竹多少次？

B I went there only once on a business trip.
我只有一次去那裡出差。

道歉

Ⓐ Yesterday you lent your bag to me. But I lost it. I am so sorry.
昨天你將你的包包借給我。但我弄丟了。我很抱歉。

Ⓑ No big deal. I have another one.
沒什麼大不了的。我還有一個。

Ⓐ That bag was a birthday gift from your mom. Are you mad at me?
這包包是你媽媽給你的生日禮物。你生我的氣嗎？

Ⓑ Not at all. Just make sure you don't do something like that in the future.
一點也不。只要確保你未來不會再做這樣的事情。

Ⓐ I will make it up to you, I promise.
我答應我會彌補你的。

Chapter 2

個人資料

Personal Information

姓名

🅐 What's your surname?
你姓什麼？

🅑 Chen.
陳。

🅐 What's your first name?
你的名字？

🅑 Daren.
大仁。

> surname 或 family name 或 last name 是姓氏。
> first name 或 given name 是名。
> 一般西方人還有中間名 middle name，華人可
> 忽略此部分。

年紀

1. Jim is 40 something, but he looks 30 something.
   吉姆40多歲,但看起來30多歲。

2. I started the business in my early 30's.
   我30出頭時開始這個事業。

說明

> mid是middle(中間)的縮寫,因此in my mid 30's表示 34,35,36 歲左右。同理,in my late 30's表示 37,38,39 歲左右。

3. Why can't I see this movie? I am already over 18 years old.
   為什麼我不能看這部電影?我已經超過18歲。

4. Daniel is a young man under 35.
   丹尼爾是一個不到35歲的年輕男子。

5. At the age of 25, I bought my first car.
   在25歲的時候,我買了我的第一輛車。

年齡聯絡方式

A What's your age?
您的年齡？

B 35.

35。

A Where are you from?
你是哪裡人？

B Houston, Texas.
德克薩斯州，休士頓市。

A Please tell us your contact
information.
請告訴我們您的聯絡方式。

B My phone number is 543-9876.
My address is 12 Apple Road.
我的電話號碼是 543-9876。
地址是蘋果路 12 號。

A Area code and zip code?
電話的區域號碼？郵遞區號？

婚姻狀況出生日期出生地

A What's your marital status?
你的婚姻狀況？

B Married.
已婚。

說明

婚姻狀況也可能是離婚divorced, 單身single, 分居separated, 也可回答prefer not to say不想說。

A Please tell us your date of birth.
請告訴我們您的出生日期。

B 23 May 1979.
1979 年 5 月 23 日。

A Your place of birth?
您的出生地？

B Tainan, Taiwan.
台灣台南。

性別種族國籍

Ⓐ This is a form about your personal info. Please fill in your gender and race.

這表格是關於您的個人資料。請填寫您的性別和種族。

Ⓑ OK. My gender is male. Talking about my race, I am Asian.

我的性別是男性。　說到種族，我是亞洲人。

Ⓐ What's your citizenship?

你的國籍是？

Ⓑ Taiwan , R.O.C.

台灣，中華民國。

說明

性別的英文也可用sex。女性是female。
國籍也可用nationality。
info就是information--資料或訊息。

成長

1. Where were you born?
   你在哪裡出生？

2. Where did you grow up?
   你在哪裡長大？

3. When did you leave your birthplace?
   你何時離開你的出生地？

4. What's your native language?
   你的母語是什麼？

5. Tell me more about your hometown.
   告訴我更多關於你的家鄉。

6. Where did you go to elementary school?
   你在哪裡唸小學？

小學的另一種說法是primary school。

第二故鄉

Ⓐ Where are you from originally?
你最初從哪裡來？

Ⓑ I am originally from Singapore. I came
to Taiwan 10 years ago. So I consider
Taiwan as my second hometown.
我最初來自新加坡。10年前來到台灣。所
以，我認為台灣是我的第二故鄉。

Ⓐ Do you enjoy working here?
你喜歡在這裡工作？

Ⓑ Of course! I will probably live here for
the rest of my life.
當然！很可能我的餘生都會住在這裡。

rest是其餘的。例如：The rest of the students
take the school bus. ------其餘的學生坐校
車。

形容人的外貌

1. She has a nice figure. She also has a pretty face.
   她有一個很好的身材，也有一個漂亮的臉蛋。

2. The lady in blue is slim but not too skinny.
   穿藍色的女士身材苗條，但不至於瘦到皮包骨。

3. Joe is a muscular guy. He works out a lot.
   喬是一個肌肉發達的傢伙。他常運動。

4. Have a flabby stomach? Daily exercise will get rid of the flab around your waist.
   腰部有贅肉？每天運動將讓你腰部甩掉贅肉。

5. I have a beer belly. Maybe it's time for bodybuilding.
   我有一個啤酒肚。也許是該健身的時候。

6. I don't care that much about figure.
   我沒有很在乎身材。

MEMO

Chapter 3

人際關係

Relationships

親屬

1. What's the name of your spouse?
   你的配偶名字是？

2. John is my uncle on my mother's side.
   約翰是我的舅舅 (屬於母親這邊)。

3. Tim is my uncle on my father's side.
   提姆是我的叔叔 (或伯父，屬於父親這邊)。

4. Joan is my aunt on my mother's side.
   瓊是我的阿姨 (屬於母親這邊)。

5. Mary is my aunt on my father's side.
   瑪麗是我的姑姑 (屬於父親這邊)。

6. Emily is my adopted daughter.
   艾蜜莉是我領養的女兒。

親屬 2

1. I totally got 4 siblings.
   我總共有4個兄弟姐妹。

> sibling是兄弟姊妹(不分男女)。

2. The name of my elder brother is Joseph.
   我哥哥的名字是約瑟夫。

3. The name of my younger brother is Joel.
   我弟弟的名字是喬爾。

4. The name of my elder sister is Julie.
   我姐姐的名字是朱莉。

5. The name of my younger sister is Marilyn.
   我妹妹的名字是瑪麗蓮。

親屬 3

1. I have a nephew and a niece. Both are 15 years old.
   我有一個侄子，一個侄女。兩個都是 15 歲。

> nephew是兄弟或姊妹的兒子，因此可指侄子或外甥。
> niece是兄弟或姊妹的女兒，因此可指侄女或外甥女。

2. My step-father is German-Irish. He also has many relatives.
   我的繼父是德國和愛爾蘭混血。他也有很多親戚。

3. My mother-in-law is 75 years of age.
   我的岳母親75歲。

> mother-in-law可指岳母或婆婆。
> father-in-law可指岳父或公公。

親屬 4

1. My wife Jessica has 5 cousins.
   我的妻子潔西卡有5個堂兄弟姊妹或表兄弟姊妹。

說明

> uncle 或 aunt 的小孩都是 cousin (不分男女)。

2. Please tell us the name of your next of kin.
   請告訴我們您最近血親的姓名。

說明

> 所謂 "最近的血親 (next of kin)" 可按一等親或二等親進行排序。

3. I am from a big family.
   我來自一個大家庭。

婚禮

A When is your wedding day?
何時是你結婚的日子？

B We haven't set the exact date, but it will be sometime in October.
我們沒有設定確切的日期，但它會在十月某個時候。

A What does he do for a living?
他做什麼工作的？

B He makes a living selling cars
賣車。

A How did he propose to you?
他是怎麼向你求婚？

B You can never imagine how romantic he was!
你永遠無法想像他有多浪漫！

嫁娶訂婚

1. Are you still together?
   你們是否還在一起？

2. Helen was married to Adam.
   海倫嫁給了亞當。

> 英文中 "嫁" 和 "娶" 都是用marry。

3. Sofia and Leon are engaged.
   索非亞和李昂訂婚。

4. Kenny's fiancée is Canadian.
   肯尼的未婚妻是加拿大人。

5. Nicole's fiancé is a teacher.
   妮可的未婚夫是一名教師。

感情發展

1. Did you ask her out?
   你約她出去了嗎？

2. I am only 28, I don't want to settle down.
   我才28歲，不想安定下來。

3. When is your big day?
   你結婚的大日子是何時？

4. Will you invite me to your wedding ceremony?
   你將邀請我參加你的婚禮嗎？

5. If you and Jane don't work out. I know another girl.
   如果你和珍沒交往成功。我認識另一個女孩。

說明

work out除了 "成功"，也有 "運動" 的意思。例如：I work out a lot----我常運動。

結婚五十周年

Ⓐ What's your plan this afternoon?
你今天下午有什麼計劃嗎？

Ⓑ I am gonna do some shopping, I have to buy some presents for my grandparents.
我要去購物，我要買禮物給我的祖父母。

Ⓐ What's the occasion?
什麼情況下的禮物？

Ⓑ It's their 50th wedding anniversary. Some call it a "golden anniversary".
這是他們結婚 50 週年紀念日。有人稱之為 "金婚"。

Ⓐ Wow! That's so great. They must have been a happy couple. I gotta go. Take care.
哇！這真是太棒了。他們一定一直都是幸福的一對。我得走了。保重。

懷孕

Ⓐ Guess what? I'm having a baby!
你猜怎麼著？我懷孕了！

Ⓑ Great. Congratulations.
太好了。恭喜！

Ⓐ My hubby and I are so excited. We kept talking about buying the baby things ahead of time.
我的丈夫和我都非常興奮。我們一直在談論先去買小孩的東西。

Ⓑ Yeah, There are lots of stuff you have to prepare for.
是啊，有很多東西你必須做好準備。

Ⓐ I know I am going to be busy, but I know I can handle it.
我知道我將會很忙，但我知道我能應付得來。

說明

hubby就是husband，丈夫。

交男女朋友

A Is your younger brother seeing someone?
你弟弟有沒有女朋友？

B I heard that he is dating a flight attendant from New Zealand.
我聽說他有和一個鈕西蘭的空姐交往。

A Is that a serious relationship?
交往關係是認真的？

B My brother told me so. However, he also said she is very sensitive and often got hurt too easily.
我弟弟說是的。不過，他也表示她很敏感，經常太容易受到傷害。

A Is it possible he might break up with her?
他可能會和她分手？

B I am not that nosy.
我沒有那麼好管閒事。

交男女朋友 2

1. I don't like pushy girls! You?
   我不喜歡強勢的女孩！你呢？

2. Looks like we have something in common.
   看來我們有共同之處。

3. She made me feel like dancing.
   她讓我想要跳舞。

4. It seems to me she is very obsessed with you.
   在我看來，她很迷戀你。

5. My relationship with Joanne? Well, so far so good.
   我與喬安妮的關係如何？嗯，目前為止一切順利。

6. Dan is very attractive. He has a nice build.
   丹很迷人。他的身材鍛鍊得很好。

交男女朋友 3

1. Larry is always wearing cologne. But honestly, I don't like that smell.
   賴瑞總是擦古龍水。不過說實話，我不喜歡那種味道。

2. She is gentle, kind and good-looking. Who can ask for more?
   她溫柔，善良又好看。你能要求更多嗎？

3. How can I forget that evening? We sat by the river and cuddled.
   我怎能忘記那天傍晚？我們坐在河邊輕輕擁抱。

4. What night to remember! He finally asked me to dance.
   多麼值得記住的夜晚！他終於開口約我跳舞。

5. How embarrassing! She stood up and walked out on me.
   多尷尬！她站起來，轉身就走。

交男女朋友 4

Ⓐ How was your date with Sandra?
你與桑德拉的約會如何？

Ⓑ We went to dinner together on Sunday.
我們週日一起吃晚餐。

Ⓐ What's her response to your invitation?
她對你的邀請如何回應？

Ⓑ She said maybe after she gets to know me better.
她說也許等她更了解我以後再說。

Ⓐ What do I talk about?
我該說甚麼？

Ⓑ Don't be too nervous. Just act naturally and be yourself!
不要太緊張。只要行動自然，做你自己！

交男女朋友 5

1. A tall, dark, handsome guy----it's many young girls' dream.
   身材高大、皮膚黝黑的帥哥----這是很多年輕女孩的夢想。

2. How long have you been looking for your Mr. Right?
   你尋找你的真命天子有多久了？

3. I don't have to live up to anyone's expectations.
   我活著不是為了達到任何人的期望。

4. John said Candice was his significant other. But I think it's not right to keep things vague.
   約翰說坎蒂絲是他的長期夥伴。但我認為這樣讓事情保持模糊是不對的。

說明

> significant other可指配偶或長期男女朋友，是一種不願正式表態的說法。

交男女朋友 6

1. I can't stand it no more. She makes selfies at least 300 times per day!
   我再也不能忍受了。她每天至少自拍300次！

2. My relationship status? I prefer not to say.
   我的感情狀態？我不想說。

3. I used to love him, but not anymore.
   我以前愛他，但現在不了。

4. What happened to me and Tracy? It's a long story.
   我和崔西間發生了什麼事？說來話長。

5. Barbara just ended a serious relationship.
   芭芭拉剛結束了一段認真的交往關係。

6. I never sent her roses before. Now I will give it a shot.
   我從沒送過她玫瑰花。現在我想嘗試看看。

交男女朋友 7

1. He is flirting with my friend. How can he do this to me?
   他正和我的朋友調情。他怎能這樣對我?

2. If I don't ask her out to lunch, someone else will.
   如果我不約她出去吃午飯,別人也會約。

3. Look at that old couple. They still have candlelit dinner together.How romantic!
   看那對老夫妻。他們仍然在一起享用燭光晚餐。多浪漫!

4. We're made for each other.
   我們是天生的一對。

5. Hey! I am not that kind of girl.
   嘿!我不是那種女孩。

6. I can survive without him.
   沒有他我照樣可以生存。

交男女朋友 8

1. I don't care about your appearance that much.
   我沒那麼在乎你的外表。

2. Who's chasing who? I am just curious about it.
   誰追誰？我只是好奇。

3. Lots of guys have a crush on her.
   很多男生都迷戀她。

4. You want me to walk you home or drive you home?
   你要我陪你走回家或開車送你回家？

5. It's very comfortable talking to you. When can I see you again?
   和你談話非常舒服。我何時才能再見到你？

6. Here's my number. Give me a call.
   這是我的號碼。打電話給我。

交男女朋友 9

A I overheard you got a new boy friend.
Where did you and he first meet?
我無意間聽到你有一個新的男朋友。你在哪裡和他第一次見面？

B He asked me for directions.
他像我問路。

A What is his personality?
他的個性如何？

B He is outgoing, friendly, reliable and honest.
他是外向的，友好的，可靠的和誠實的。

A Does he do household chores often?
他是不是常做家事？

B His home is always clean and tidy.
他的家總是乾淨整潔。

交男女朋友 10

A What's going on?
你好嗎？

說明

> What's going on?可指 "發生什麼事" ，或者
> 單純當作招呼用語。

B Nothing special.
沒什麼特別的。

A Have you found a boy friend yet?
How about that guy from work?
找到男朋友了？工作場合的那男孩呢？

B Turns out he already has a girl friend.
原來他已經有了女朋友。

說明

> Turn out是近來很流行的英文片語，可翻成
> "原來" 或 "結果發現" 或 "結果證明" 。

交男女朋友 11

A What's wrong?
哪裡不對？

B I just broke up with my girlfriend.
我剛和女友分手。

A Come on. It's not the end of the world. You have to move on.
拜託。這不是世界末日。你必須繼續前進。

B I know. But it takes time to recover. I still miss her so much.
我知道。但是這需要時間復原。我仍然很想念她。

A Trust me. You'll find someone again. Someone deserves your love.
相信我。你會再找到一個值得你愛的人。

B To look on the bright side, I have lots of freedom now.
看光明面，我現在有很多的自由了。

交男女朋友 12

Ⓐ You're so busy recently. Are you dating someone?
你最近這麼忙。你有交往對象？

Ⓑ Remember the girl we met a couple of weeks ago?
還記得我們幾個星期前遇到的女孩嗎？

Ⓐ I like the one in the green T-shirt.
我喜歡穿綠色 T 恤的那個。

Ⓑ You gotta be kidding me! She is 10 years younger than you.
你肯定在開玩笑吧！她比你年輕10歲。

Ⓐ I enjoy chatting with you.
我喜歡和你聊天。

Ⓑ I feel the same way.
我有同樣的感覺。

交男女朋友 13

1. I suggest you make up with Jody.
   我建議你和茱蒂和好。

2. I don't want to go out with Johnny anymore.
   我不想再和強尼出去了。

3. Can someone teach me how to turn down his invitation? I don't have the heart to hurt him.
   有沒有人能教我如何拒絕他的邀請？我不想傷害他。

4. I didn't dump her, she dumped me!
   我沒有拋棄她，她把我甩了！

5. She didn't want to shake hands with my new girl friend.
   她不想和我的新女友握手。

6. Please come back. Just give me one more chance.
   請回來。再給我一次機會。

與網友見面

🅐 You should be careful when finding friends on the Internet.
在網路上交朋友時應謹慎。

🅑 I agree. I always use a nickname when chatting online.
我同意。我在網上聊天時只使用暱稱。

🅐 Never give out personal information including age, address, and so on.
永遠不要把年齡住址等個人訊息公開。

🅑 Can I meet him if he asks me out?
如果他約我，我可以和他出去嗎？

🅐 Make sure it is in a public place.
請確定是在公共場所見面。

🅑 Thanks for your advice.
謝謝你的建議。

與網友見面 2

A Let's go out and have some fun.
讓我們出去找一些好玩的事。

B I have something pressing now.
我現在有一些急事。

A Maybe we can hang out together some other time.
也許我們改天可以一起出去。

B Yup, maybe.
是啊，也許吧。

A Do you have plans for the weekend?
你這週末有何計劃？

B What a coincidence! My mom is coming.
真是太巧了！我媽媽要來。

MEMO

Chapter 4

傳遞訊息

Messages

電話

1. **A** This is Mike speaking. May I speak to Mr. Brown, please.
   我是麥克，請接布朗先生。

   B One moment please.
   請稍後，

2. **A** Hold the line, I will put you through to extension 223.
   請勿掛斷，我將幫你轉接分機223。

   B No one answered the phone.
   沒人接。

   A Maybe he is out for lunch.
   也許他外出午餐。

   B I will call again.
   我會再打來。

電話 2

A I am calling to inquire about the bus schedule.
我想詢問巴士時刻表。

B Hold on a second.
請稍後。

A Thank you for calling IBM. How may I help you?
這裏是 IBM 公司，有甚麼可為你服務的嗎？

B Is Michael Smith in?
麥可史密斯在嗎？

A I will transfer your call. Don't hang up.
我將幫你轉接，請勿掛斷。

A The line is busy. Would you like to leave a message?
忙線中，你想留訊息給他嗎？

電話 3

A Don't text and drive!
不可邊開車邊發簡訊。

B I know it's against the law.
我知道這是違法的。

A What are the calling hours for technical support?
我何時可打來尋求技術支援？

B From 10:00 AM to 10:00 PM.
從上午10點到下午10點。

A I am calling to cancel the reservation.
我打電話來取消預約。

B You have reached the wrong number.
你撥了錯誤的號碼。

電話 4

A Hi Amy, it's Doug. Did you get my message?
嗨艾美，我是道格。你有收到我的消息嗎？

B Yes, I tried to call you back.
是的，我有試著回你電話。

A Sorry, I was busy cooking when you called.
抱歉，當你打來時我正忙著做飯。

B Then I called again at night.
我晚上又打了一次。

A I always turn my cell phone off after 7 PM.
我一向晚上7點以後把手機關機。

B I understand that.
我了解。

電話 5

A May I speak to John?
約翰在嗎？

B Who's calling please?
請問你是？

A I am his friend Gilbert.
我是他朋友吉伯特。

B Hold on please.
請稍後。

D He won't be here until 11.00 AM, can I take a message?
他早上11:00後才進來，要留訊息嗎？

A Please tell him to call me back.
請他回我電話。

電話 6

A Sorry for calling so late, did I wake you up?

對不起，這麼晚打給你，把你吵醒了嗎？

B I just finished some work. I haven't gone to bed yet.

其實，我剛完成了一些工作，還沒睡覺。

A I just want to let you know Jane passed the exam.

我想讓你知道珍通過了考試。

B Great!

太好了！

A I am so proud of her.

我很為她驕傲。

B I bet you are.

我想你是。

電話 7

Ⓐ Could I speak to the general manager?
我能總經理說話嗎？

Ⓑ He is on another line.
他在另一條線上。

Ⓐ Is the CFO in the office?
CFO 在辦公室嗎？

Ⓑ He can't come to the telephone right now.
他現在無法接聽。

Ⓐ I'm trying to contact Mr. Johnson.
我找強森先生。

Ⓑ The line is engaged.
電話忙線中。

說明

The line is engaged 和 The line is busy 都是忙線中，前者是英式用法，後者是美式用法。

電話 8

1. Hello, the Asia Hotel, Sam Leo speaking, what can I do for you?
   您好，這是亞洲大酒店。我是山姆·里歐，我能為您做點什麼？

2. OK, you'd like to make a reservation. Can I have your name, please?
   OK,你想訂房。可以給我你的名字嗎？

3. Could you tell me how to spell your name?
   可以告訴我怎麼拼你的名字嗎？

4. I'm sorry, I didn't catch your name.
   對不起，我沒聽清楚你的名字。

5. Could you repeat it, please?
   你能重複一次嗎？

6. Could you speak up?
   你能說大聲點嗎？

電話 9

1. Please dial our toll free number
   0800-333-666.
   請改撥免付費電話0800-333-666。

2. Excuse me, is your area code 212?
   對不起，你的區域號碼是212？

3. The country code of Taiwan is 886.
   台灣的國碼是886。

4. This is Lucy from XYZ International.
   I'm returning your call.
   這是 XYZ 國際公司的露西。我打來是為
   了回你電話。

5. Thanks for calling. What is it
   regarding, please?
   感謝來電。請問您的來電是關於什麼？

6. Roger is not available right now.
   羅傑現在無法接聽。

聽不清楚對方的話

1. What was that again?

2. Pardon?

3. Excuse me.
   以上三種都是麻煩對方再從新說一次。

說明

> 另外，Excuse me也可以表示"借過"。

Ⓐ Excuse me.
　　借過。

Ⓑ I am sorry.
　　抱歉擋了你的路。

說明

> Excuse me也可作為問話前的禮貌用語。
> Excuse me, where is the restroom？
> 不好意思，廁所在哪裡。

聽不清楚對方的話 2

1. Sorry, would you mind repeating that, please?
   對不起，你介意重複說一次嗎？

2. Celebrity? What does it mean? Ok, it means famous people. I got it.
   Celebrity？這是什麼意思？OK，這是指名人。我知道了。

3. I don't quite follow you
   我不太明白你的意思。

4. I don't fully understand what you said.
   我不完全理解你說什麼。

5. Trout? Is it some kind of fish?
   Trout？它是某種魚類？

6. Can you speak more slowly, please?
   你能說慢一點，好嗎？

7. McDermont? How do you spell it?
   McDermont？怎麼拼？

聽不清楚對方的話 3

A Please repeat your name slowly for me.

請慢慢的重複你的名字。

B I will spell it for you. M-i-n-g N-i-n-g Y-u.

我會拼給你聽。M-i-n-g N-i-n-g Y-u。

A Your name is Ming Ning Yu. Did I hear you right?

你的名字是明寧余。我聽對了？

B That's correct. My flight number is Alpha Kilo 339.

沒錯。我的班機號碼是 AK339。

說明

有些英文字母發音近似，例如C與D。因此在電話中通常會以另一單字取代，以避免對方誤聽。例如：A說成Alpha, B說成 Bravo，就像軍中將 170 念成"ㄠ拐洞"一樣。以下是個 26 字母完整對照表。

A Alpha B Bravo C Charlie D Delta E Echo F
Foxtrott G Golf H Hotel I India J Juliet K Kilo
L Lima M Mike N November O Oskar
P Papa Q Quebec R Romeo S Sierra T Tango U
Uniform V Victor W Whiskey
X X-Ray Y Yankee Z Zulu

上列這些不須死背，只要確定對方不會聽錯
就好。例如：G不一定要說Golf,也可說
George。

答錄機或語音信箱

A Hi, this is Lisa. I'm sorry I'm not available to take your call at this time. Leave me a message and I'll get back to you asap.

我是麗莎,很抱歉現在無法接聽您的電話,請留言,我將盡快與您聯絡。

asap 等於 as soon as possible,盡快。

B Hello Lisa. This is Helen from the post office calling. I'm not sure if you got my first message so I am leaving one more. Your package just arrived.

嗨!麗莎,我是郵局的海倫,我不確定妳是否收到了我第一個留言,所以再留一次。妳的包裹已經到了。

答錄機或語音信箱 2

A Hello. You've reached 2132-6777. We can't answer right now. Please leave a message after the beep. We'll return your call asap. If this is an emergency, please call Mr. Jackson at 2132-6788. His cell phone number is 0956-657321. Thank you.

您好，這裏是 2132-6777，現在無法接聽電話，請於嗶聲後留言，我們將盡快回您電話。如果是緊急狀況，請打給傑克森先生，電話是 2132-6788，手機是 0956-657321。

B This is Susan McCoy. Please call me back at 3124-5678.

我是蘇珊麥考依，請回我電話，電話是 3124-5678。

郵件

A I would like to send this letter to Japan.
我想寄這封信到日本。

B How would you like to send it, priority mail or regular mail?
你想用優先郵件或一般郵件？

A What is the price difference?
價格差多少？

B $1.25 for regular mail. Priority Mail prices are based on weight and zone.
普通郵件價格是1.25。優先郵件價格根據重量和區域。

A I'll send it through regular airmail.
我用普通郵件發送。

B Any food items, firearms or explosives in here?
裡面有任何食品，槍械或爆裂物？

郵件 2

A Could you pick up my mail at the office?

你可以幫我收辦公室的郵件嗎？

B Sure.

當然。

A Please bring it to my home.

請帶來我家。

B It was nothing but ads and coupons for shopping. Wait! Let me check. There're a few bills for you.

只有廣告和購物優惠券。等一下！讓我看看。這裡有一些帳單。

A From the electric company?

電力公司的？

B That's right.

是。

郵件 3

A Did you get the mail yet today?
你今天收信了嗎？

B Yes. I picked it up this morning.
是的。我早上有收。

A Was there anything for me?
有我的信嗎？

B There was only a letter from my penpal.
只有一封我筆友寄來的信。

A I am waiting for the letter from the American Embassy.
我正在等美國大使館的信。

B I know you're applying for a U.S. visa.
我知道你正在申請美國簽證。

寄送包裹

A I want to send this package to Thailand.

我想這個包裹寄到泰國。

B Would you like to send it by regular mail or express mail?

你想用普通郵件或快速郵件發送？

A I'd like it to get there in two days.

我希望兩天內能到達。

B Please fill out this form.

請填寫此表。

A I'm done, is this correct?

完成了，正確嗎？

B Yes, that's right.

是的，這是正確的。

A This item is fragile. Please handle it with care.

這個物品是易碎的。請小心處理。

提醒

A Watch out for the car!
當心車！

B Thanks. That was really close.
謝謝。真的就差一點。

A Please remind me to text David this afternoon.
今天下午請提醒我發簡訊給大衛。

B Will do. It's 10:30 am. Aren't you forgetting something?
會的。現在上午十點半，你是不是忘了什麼？

A It's time to call my son. Thanks.
現在是打電話給兒子的時候。謝謝。

A Don't forget to wake me up tomorrow morning.
不要忘記明天早上叫醒我。

B You can count on me.
你可以信賴我。

電子郵件

Please teach me about the following things.
請教我下面這些事情。

1. How do I set up an email account?
   如何建立一個電子郵件帳號？

2. How to reply to a message?
   如何回覆訊息？

3. How to forward a message?
   如何轉寄郵件？

4. How to send photos through email?
   如何透過電子郵件發送照片？

5. How to send an email to more than one person?
   如何發送電子郵件給多人？

6. How to open an attachment?
   如何打開附件？

電子郵件 2

1. The difference between "reply" and "reply all" is: "reply" only goes to the sender, but "reply all" goes to everyone who has received this email.

   "回覆"和"全部回覆"的區別是："回覆"只寄給寄件者，而是"全部回覆"寄給所有收到這封電子郵件的人。

2. When you send the files to Morris, don't forget to cc me.

   當您寄送檔案給摩里斯，不要忘了寄副本給我。

3. Don't open any mail with the title, 'YOU WON THE LOTTERY!!!'
   It contains a virus. Please delete this mail immediately if you see it.

   不要打開任何有下列標題郵件，"你贏了樂透！"。它含有病毒。如果你看到它該郵件，請立即刪除。

電子郵件 3

1. I can't access my email right now. Is it because the mail server is down?
   我無法進入我的電子郵件帳號。是不是因為郵件伺服器當機？

2. My email address is xyz@abc.com.
   我的電子郵件地址是 xyz@abc.com。

3. The file is too large to send through email.
   檔案太大，無法透過電子郵件發送。

4. We will provide you with the most up-to-date information on a daily basis.
   我們將為您提供每天最即時資訊。

5. If there are any further developments, we'll keep you posted.
   如果有任何進一步的發展，我們會通知你。

6. I sent him an email concerning his job situation.
   我寄給他一封有關他工作狀況的電子郵件。

電子郵件與書信

Dear Martha,

I am writing to apologize for the misunderstanding. I promise it will never happen again. I look forward to seeing you soon.

Sincerely,
Tom
Jan 1, 2015

親愛的瑪莎，

我對這場誤會感到抱歉， 我保證以後不會再發生了，期待能盡快與妳相見。

湯姆 敬上
2015 年 1 月 1 日

Sincerely 是信尾的禮貌用語，也可用 Best Regards 或 Best wishes 取代。

電子郵件與書信— 不知對方確實身分時

To whom it may concern:

I am pleased to write this recommendation letter for Mr. Chen. Mr. Chen is a great leader with a promising future,
Sincerely,

David Lee
General Manager
ABC, Inc

敬啟者

我很樂意為陳先生寫這封介紹信，他是一位優秀領導人，未來前景看好。

ABC 公司總經理
李大衛 上

Chapter 5

飲食

Food and Drink

對於食物的表達

1. The food is so fresh!
   食物好新鮮！

2. It tastes good.
   味道很好。

3. It's too salty.
   太鹹了。

4. They were so yummy!
   真好吃！

5. So delicious!
   真美味！

6. What a tasty fish.
   真是好吃的魚。

7. It's too sour!
   太酸了！

對於食物的表達 2

1. It tastes stale!
   這不新鮮！

2. This dish is overcooked.
   這道菜過度烹調。

說明

> dish本指盤子，但有時也可指一道菜。over
> 通常有過度的意思，因此overcooked表示煮
> 太久或經過太多處理。over的相反是under。
> 例如：The chicken is undercooked.
> 這道雞沒煮熟。

3. This mustard is really hot!
   這芥末醬真辣！

4. I am crazy about the lemon-flavored
   potato chips.
   我為那檸檬口味的洋芋片瘋狂。

飲食

1. I'm done.
   我吃完了。

說明

done表示"做完了"，例如：I am done with my homework.-----我的家庭作業寫完了。
因此，I'm done eating lunch可以簡稱I'm done，表示"吃完了"。

2. I am starving!
   我餓壞了！

說明

hungry是"普通餓"，starving比hungry更強烈。

3. I am so hungry, I could eat a cow!
   我太餓了，我可以吃下一頭牛！

飲食 2

1. I'm full.
   我吃飽了。

2. I'm so stuffed.
   我吃的好撐。

3. No more cake. I had my fill already.
   不要再來蛋糕了。我已經吃很夠了。

4. This juice smells so good!
   這種果汁聞起來真香！

5. I love these Korean side dishes!
   我愛這些韓國小菜！

6. Wow! So spicy! My mouth is on fire!
   哇！好辣！我的嘴巴著火了！

7. Beef cooked with banana? This food combination is really weird!
   牛肉煮香蕉？這種食物組合真是怪異！

飲食 3

1. I always like fermented food such as kimchi and pickles.

   我向來喜歡發酵或醃漬的食物，如泡菜和醃黃瓜。

2. A typhoon is coming. So I have bought some instant noodles and frozen mixed vegetables.

   颱風要來了。所以我已經買了一些泡麵和冷凍混合蔬菜。

3. How do you like your fish prepared? Smoked? Steamed? In a soup? Grilled? Deep fried?

   你喜歡怎麼吃你的魚？煙燻？清蒸？煮湯？烤？油炸？

4. When you go camping, it's convenient to eat some preserved food and canned food.

   當你去露營時，吃一些被瓶裝醃製保存的食品和罐頭食品是很方便的。

飲食 4

1. Sabrina is a very thrifty person. She always brings leftover food home from restaurants.
   薩布麗娜是一個非常節儉的人。她總是從餐館把吃剩的食物帶回家。

2. What sweets do you like to eat the most?
   你最喜歡吃什麼糖果？

> sweets, candy都是糖果，例如棒棒糖、巧克力糖、薄荷糖等。sweets是英式用法，candy是美式用法。

3. Care for some tacos?
   想來點墨西哥脆餅嗎？

> "care for＋名詞"與 "care to＋動詞"都是喜歡。
> 例句：I really don't care to see that soap opera.
> 我真的不喜歡看那部肥皂劇。

飲食 5

1. Where are the napkins? I have BBQ sauce all over my face.
   餐巾在哪裡？我滿臉烤肉醬。

2. I like to dine at Star café because the atmosphere is always right.
   我喜歡在明星餐館用餐，因為氣氛永遠是對的。

3. The school deli has Swedish décor.
   學校熟食店有瑞典風格的裝潢。

deli是賣三明治等輕食的地方。

4. In Taiwan, there are lots of night markets in both urban and suburban areas.
   在台灣的城市和郊區都有很多夜市。

5. This tomato soup is very thick.
   這番茄湯很濃。

飲食 6

1. Teach me how to prepare a no hassle meal!
   教我如何準備省錢、不麻煩、不費時的一餐！

2. It costs me so much money to dine out every day.
   天天外食花了我很多錢。

3. I have to whip up a meal for them.
   我必須為他們匆匆準備一餐。

4. Please name 5 happy mood foods.
   請說出5種讓心情愉快的食物。

5. Try adding a spoonful of honey to your tea.
   嘗試加入一匙蜂蜜在你的茶。

說明

類似spoonful的字還有mouthful與handful，例如：I only ate a mouthful of food--我只吃一口食物。He grabbed a handful of coins---他抓了一把零錢。

飲食 7

1. She'll be glad if we eat up all the food on the table.
   她會很高興如果我們吃光所有桌上的食物。

2. I like to drink up all the guava juice.
   我想喝光所有的芭樂汁。

3. Shall we order in some lunch boxes?
   我們應該外叫一些餐盒進來？

4. Do you want to eat in or eat out tonight?
   你想今晚想在家吃或吃外面？

5. It's a snack between meals.
   這是兩餐之間的點心。

6. Don't forget to buy a can opener.
   不要忘了買一個開罐器。

7. That's disgusting!
   那樣真噁心！

餐廳

Ⓐ May I take your order, please?
我可以為你點餐嗎？

Ⓑ Yes, we're ready.
是的，我們準備好了。

Ⓐ What are you going to have?
想點甚麼？

Ⓑ I'd like the seafood spaghetti.
我想要海鮮義大利麵。

Ⓐ Would you like anything for dessert?
想吃飯後甜點嗎？

Ⓑ Blueberry pie.
藍莓派。

Ⓐ How's everything?
餐點還好嗎？

餐廳 2

Ⓐ Do you want me to share my chicken wings with you?
你想分享我的雞翅嗎？

Ⓑ Sure, could you pass the salt and the pepper, please?
當然，你可以將鹽和胡椒遞給我嗎？

Ⓐ Here you are.
給你。

Ⓐ I ordered too many French fries. You want some?
我點了太多的薯條。你想分一些嗎？

Ⓑ No, thank you. I have enough food already. Would you like some of my salad?
不用了，謝謝，我有足夠的食物了，你想分一些我的沙拉嗎？

Ⓐ OK. Just a little bit.
一點點就好。

餐廳 3

Ⓐ Can I see a menu, please?
我可以看菜單嗎？

Ⓑ Certainly, here you are.
當然可以，給你。

Are you ready to order?
您準備點菜了嗎？

Ⓐ Yes, what's today's special?
是的，今日特餐是什麼？

Ⓑ Grilled sirloin steak.
烤沙朗牛排。

Ⓐ That sounds good. I'll have that.
聽起來不錯。我就點這個。

Ⓑ Would you like anything to drink?
想喝點甚麼嗎？

餐廳 4

A What would you like to order? Wanna
try our combo meals?
請問您想點甚麼？想試我們的組合餐？

B I'll take number 2.
我要2號餐。

A Will that be all?
還要別的嗎？

B I will also have a chocolate milkshake.
我也要一個巧克力奶昔。

A For here or to go?
內用或外帶？

B For here.
內用。

A The total comes to \$4.35.
總共4.35元。

餐廳 5

🅐 Looks like you and the waiter are good friends.
看起來你和服務員是好朋友。

🅑 I am a regular at this café.
我是這家餐廳的常客。

🅐 So, what would you recommend me to order?
所以，你建議我點甚麼？

🅑 You might wanna try the roast chicken here. It's mouthwatering.
你可能會想嘗試這裡的烤雞。這是令人垂涎三尺的。

說明

名詞加動名詞合成一個字是一種常見的形容詞用法，mouthwatering 意思是這個食物會 water your mouth (讓你口中充滿口水)。同理，fingers-licking good 表示這個食物好吃到會讓你 lick your fingers (舔你的手指)。

餐廳 6

A Welcome to Redwood restaurant.
Today's special is smoked salmon.
歡迎來到紅木餐廳，今日特餐是煙燻鮭魚。

B I'm still trying to decide.
我還沒決定要點甚麼。

A I'll be back shortly.
我待會再過來。

A Can I take your order now?
現在可以點餐了嗎？

B I'll have a hamburger and fries.
給我漢堡與薯條。

A Will there be anything else?
還需要其它的嗎？

B No, that's all.
這就夠了。

餐廳 7

1. Wanna try our aperitifs infused with herbs?
   想試試我們用草藥浸泡的開胃酒？

2. Sherry often eats salad as a main course.
   雪莉常將沙拉當主菜吃。

主菜的英文是 main course 或 main dish。

3. I am very fond of meat seasoned with salt and pepper.
   我很喜歡用鹽和胡椒調味的肉類。

4. Do you like to eat Chinese or Korean?
   你喜歡吃中國菜還是韓國菜？

5. Can you pass me the tomato sauce?
   你可以把番茄醬遞給我嗎？

餐廳 8

1. Do you offer catering service for ban-quets?
   你們提供宴會餐飲服務？

2. Look at all these exquisite appetizers!
   看看這些精美的開胃菜！

3. We ate a la carte.
   我們吃單點菜色。

> a la carte是從法文來的，意指非組合餐或套餐的單點菜色。

5. May I have a veggie sandwich?
   可以給我一個素食三明治？

> veggie是vegetarian的簡稱。

餐廳 9

A I didn't order smoked salmon. The squid is not fresh.
我沒有點煙燻鮭魚。魷魚不新鮮。

B I am terribly sorry, sir.
很對不起，先生。

A Do you offer delivery service?
你們提供外送服務嗎？

B Yup, please inform us your designated place and time.
是啊，請告訴我們您指定的時間和地點。

A Do you want separate bills?
你們想要分別的賬單 (各付各的意思)？

B Why bother?
何必麻煩呢？

餐廳 10

1. Rosy restaurant has excellent Italian cuisine.
   玫瑰餐廳擁有一流的意大利料理。

2. The title of the book is gourmet paradise.
   這本書的名字是美食天堂。

3. I am not into fast food.
   我對速食不感興趣。

4. The supper is on me.
   晚餐我請。

5. Please have a cup of coffee on the house.
   請喝杯免費招待的咖啡。

6. It's my treat.
   我請客。

7. Let us drink to you and your future wife!
   讓我們舉杯祝福你和你未來的妻子！

餐廳 11

Ⓐ How would you like your steak?
你喜歡如何吃你的牛排？

Ⓑ Well done.
全熟

說明

Medium 五分熟， Medium Well 七八分熟，
Well done 全熟。

Ⓐ Could I get a refill?
我可以續杯？

Ⓑ Of course, help yourself, please.
當然，請自行取用。

說明

"re＋動詞" 有 "重新再一次" 的意思，例
如：redo＝重做一次。 reconsider＝重新考
慮。 fill 本意是 "加滿"，refill 就是重新加
滿，也就是續杯。

餐廳 12

1. I am a Cantonese food lover. I eat dim sum and chow mein every week.
   我是一個廣東美食愛好者。我每星期都吃港式點心和炒麵。

2. It's always cheaper to order a combo meal.
   訂購組合餐總是更便宜的。

說明

combo meal (組合餐)就像漢堡搭配薯條和可樂。類似的英文還有 set meal (套餐)---例如，炒飯加貢丸湯與中杯飲料。

3. You can find lots of snacks and quick meals in a food court.
   在美食廣場你可發現很多點心和快餐。

4. We have only 30 minutes for lunch. I hope they offer some grab-and-go food.
   我們只有 30 分鐘吃午餐。我希望他們提供一些買了就走的食品。

餐廳 13

1. My friend will have lamb chop. I'll have the same.
   我的朋友點羊排，我也一樣。

2. Enjoy your meal! You can ring the bell for service.
   請享用你的餐點，如需服務請按鈴。

3. My favorite salad dressing is Caesar's.
   我最喜歡的沙拉醬是凱薩。

4. No, I don't need anything else. Just the bill please.
   不，我不需要再點別的東西。請把帳單給我就好。

5. We can customize your meal. Please tell us your meal selections.
   我們可以客製化你的餐點。請告訴我們您的用餐選擇。

6. Can you add more toppings on my pizza?
   可以在我的披薩上多加配料嗎？

餐廳 14

A Could I get the bill, please.
請給我帳單。

說明

買單也可說成 I'd like the check，或只說
check, please。

B OK, how was everything?
一切都好嗎？

A I am very pleased with your food and service.
我很滿意你們的食物與服務。

B Would you like this to-go?
這個要打包嗎？

A Yes, can you put it in a plastic bag?
是的，可以用塑膠袋裝嗎？

B Sure, no problem.
當然，沒問題。

外叫披薩

A This is Bravo Pizza. How may I help you?

這裡是 Bravo 披薩，有甚麼可為你服務的嗎？

B I'd like to order a pizza.

我要訂一個披薩。

A What size and flavor would you like?

你想要甚麼尺寸和口味？

B A medium Hawaiian.

中的夏威夷。

A Anything else?

還要其他的嗎？

B Two bottles of coke, two baskets of fried chicken, 3 garlic bread, 2 salad boxes with Italian style tuna.

兩瓶可樂，兩籃炸雞，三個大蒜麵包，兩盒義式風味鮪魚沙拉。

飯後甜點

Ⓐ A dessert would be a perfect ending to our dinner.

對我們的晚餐而言，甜品將是一個完美的結局。

Ⓑ What do you have in mind?

那你有什麼想法？

Ⓐ I am thinking of a strawberry pie. How about you?

我想要草莓派。你呢？

說明

> berry是莓，常見的還有cranberry (小紅莓), blueberry (藍莓)等。

Ⓑ Exactly the same!

完全一樣！

Ⓐ Usually, apple pie is my favorite. But I ate too many apples yesterday.

通常，蘋果派是我的最愛。但我昨天吃了太多的蘋果。

野餐

A What are you doing tomorrow?
明天你打算做什麼？

B Nothing really.
其實沒什麼事。

A I am having a cookout party. You wanna come over?
我要來個戶外野炊。你想參加？

B Why not! I will prepare salads.
為什麼不！我會準備沙拉。

A Do you remember we had a picnic on the beach 5 years ago?
你還記得5年前我們在海灘野餐嗎？

B Of course. You brought a lot of junk food.
當然。你帶了很多垃圾食物。

A You just drank milk and ate sandwi-ches.
你只喝牛奶吃三明治。

微波食品

🅐 Let's go out to grab something to eat!
我們出去隨便找點東西吃吧！

🅑 I have some spaghetti in the fridge. It's already cooked. All I have to do is to nuke it.
我有一些意大利麵在冰箱裡。已經煮熟。我只要用微波爐加熱就好。

說明

fridge是refrigerator的縮寫，也就是冰箱。

說明

nuke本來是指nuclear，也就是和核能有關的事物。但在英文中nuke也表示用微波爐加熱食物。

🅐 Indeed, microwaving is the most convenient way to heat up food.
真的，微波爐是加熱食物最方便的方式。

食譜

A How do you like the chicken?
你喜歡這道雞肉嗎？

B It's really tasty. Did you cook it your-self?
這真是好吃。你自己煮的嗎？

A I made it this morning.
我今天上午做的。

B Where did you get the recipe?
你從哪兒弄來的食譜？

A My mom passed it down to me. By the way, you should try our home made pie next time.
我媽媽傳給我的。附帶一提，你下一次應該嚐嚐我們的自製派。

B I can't wait!
我等不及了！

喝酒

A How often do you drink?
你多常喝酒？

B It depends on my mood.
看我的心情。

A How much do you usually drink?
你通常喝多少？

B Most of the time, 3 beers, don't wanna get too drunk.
在大多數情況下，3罐啤酒，不想太醉。

A I understand. A hangover might give you a headache.
我了解，宿醉可能給你頭痛。

B I am not an alcoholic.
我不是一個酒鬼。

Chapter 6

服裝、鞋子、配件

Clothing, Shoes, Accessories

服裝、鞋子、配件

A I just lost some weight. It seems I need skirts in smaller sizes.
我剛減了一些體重。看來我需要更小尺寸的裙子。

B These items are on clearance. You can buy them for half price.
這些項目都在出清。你可以用半價購買。

A I don't know what my size is now, can you take my measurement?
我不知道我現在的尺寸，你可以幫我測量？

B No problem. I will help you to get the right size.
沒問題。我會幫助你找到正確的尺寸。

A Where is your dressing room?
你們的更衣室在哪裡？

B Right over there.
就在那邊。

服裝、鞋子、配件 2

A I am looking for a shirt.
我在找一件襯衫。

B What size do you wear?
你穿什麼尺寸？

A Large, I think.
大的，我想。

B How does it fit?
它合身嗎？

A It's still a bit small for me. Do you have an extra large?
它仍然有點小。你們有 XL (加大)的嗎？

B Please wait a minute. I will bring your size out to you. Do you prefer a plain shirt or a striped shirt?
請等一下。我去把你的尺寸拿出來給你。
你喜歡素面或條紋的？

A Perhaps a plaid shirt is fine.
或許格子的好了。

服裝、鞋子、配件 3

A I need to purchase men's blue jeans.
我要買男生的牛仔褲。

B Please follow me. What size are you?
請跟我來。你是什麼尺寸？

A I'm a medium.
我穿中號。

B Would you also like to take some pairs of pants?
你是否也想買一些褲子？

說明

pairs of pants----因為褲子有兩條褲管，所以英文會加上 pair (一雙)。

A Only blue jeans. Blue jeans never become out of date.
只買牛仔褲。牛仔褲永不退流行。

服裝、鞋子、配件 4

A My I try this coat on?
我可以試穿這件外套嗎？

B Certainly! It makes you look so gorgeous!
當然！它會讓你看起來很漂亮！

A Where's the fitting room?
試衣間在哪裡？

B On second floor.
在二樓。

A It's too tight for me.
太緊了。

B We have jackets, too.
我們也有夾克。

A Zippers or buttons?
拉鍊式或鈕扣式？

服裝、鞋子、配件 5

1. She will teach you how to mix and match accessories.
   她會教你如何混搭配件。

2. Your belt goes very well with your trousers.
   您的皮帶和你的褲子搭配得很好。

3. This casual shirt doesn't fit.
   這休閒衫不合身。

4. Can I find the kind of shoes without laces?
   你們有賣不綁鞋帶的鞋子？

5. You can exchange this dress with anything of the same price.
   您可以用這件衣服交換同價位的任何商品。

說明

通常dress是指女生連身式的衣服。

服裝、鞋子、配件 6

1. I wear a size eight and a half.
   我穿八號半。

2. Can you get me a pair of high heel shoes?
   您能否給我一雙高跟鞋？

3. That bracelet looks so cute.
   這手鐲看起來很可愛。

4. I bought this ring at the jewelry store downtown.
   我在市中心珠寶店買了這個戒指。

5. I love this sportswear on you.
   這運動服穿在妳身上很棒。

6. You look great in that suit.
   你穿那套西裝很好看。

7. These gloves keep me warm.
   這手套讓我溫暖。

服裝、鞋子、配件7

1. What did you wear to John's high school graduation?
   你穿甚麼去參加約翰的高中畢業典禮？

2. I feel like doing some shopping for new clothes.
   我想要購物一些新衣服。

3. We need formal clothes for business meetings.
   我們需要穿正式服裝參加商務會議。

4. How would you dress for such an important occasion?
   這麼重要的場合你會如何穿著？

5. All these suits were tailor-made.
   所有這些西裝都是量身訂做的。

說明

tailor-made等於 custom-made。

服裝、鞋子、配件 8

1. Everybody wears a mask to join that masquerade.
   每個人都戴著面具參加那場化裝舞會。

2. She always wears a surgical mask when visiting public places.
   她前往公共場所時總是戴著口罩。

3. That article teaches you how to dress like a New Yorker.
   那文章教你如何打扮的像一個紐約客。

4. Are you attracted to those women's fancy belts?
   你是否被那些女用花俏腰帶吸引？

5. Kids are naughty sometimes, so they need sturdy clothes.
   孩子有時很調皮，因此需要耐磨的衣服。

> sturdy 是強壯或堅固的意思，例如：sturdy athlete-----強壯的運動員。

服裝、鞋子、配件 9

1. That pair of boots were made in Italy.
   那雙靴子是意大利製。

2. I love that pair of white socks with pink stars.
   我愛那雙白色有粉紅色星星圖案的襪子。

3. Do you think this blouse is pretty?
   你認為這件女性上衣漂亮嗎？

4. I like to wear slippers at home.
   我在家喜歡穿拖鞋。

5. Flip flops are very popular in Taiwan.
   夾腳拖在台灣很受歡迎。

6. He will teach you how to match neckties to your suits.
   他會教你如何搭配領帶與西裝。

7. He bought a new leather wallet.
   他買了一個新的皮夾。

服裝、鞋子、配件 10

1. That handbag was her birthday gift.
   這手提包是她的生日禮物。

2. What's the use of buying a swimsuit
   for her? She is afraid of water!
   買泳衣給她有什麼用？她怕水！

3. Did you see my dad? He is wearing
   sunglasses and athletic shoes.
   你有沒有看到我的爸爸？他戴墨鏡和穿運
   動鞋。

4. It's freezing outside, and you're wearing shorts!
   現在外面冰凍，你還穿短褲！

5. Vests are sleeveless.
   背心是無袖的。

說明

英文字加上 less 就是 "沒有" 的意思。例
如：wireless 無線、 homeless 無家可歸、
careless 不小心等等。

服裝 · 鞋子 · 配件 11

1. Purple doesn't look good on you.
   你穿紫色不好看。

2. My shoes are dirty, I will take them off.
   我的鞋子髒了，我要脫掉他們。

3. It's getting colder, please put on your coat.
   天氣越來越冷，請穿上外套。

4. That salesman likes you. Perhaps you'll be able to talk down the price.
   那業務員喜歡你。也許你能將價格壓低。

5. You'd better wrap up before going out.
   你最好穿暖和些再出去。

wrap up 和 bundle up 意思一樣，指全身包起來。

服裝、鞋子、配件 12

1. This is a formal meeting. Please button up your shirt.
   這是一個正式會議。請將你的襯衫扣好。

2. Everybody dressed up to attend that party.
   每個人都盛裝出席了派對。

3. Your parents are coming. Why don't you sort out your clothes?
   你的父母要來了。你為什麼不整理你的衣服？

4. Your garment indeed caught my eye.
   你的衣服確實吸引了我的目光。

5. Finally, he decided to save money up to buy that pair of boots.
   最後，他決定省錢買那雙靴子。

6. Dr. Smith is not picky about clothes.
   史密斯博士對衣服不挑剔。

服裝、鞋子、配件 13

1. Don't put money in your back pockets.
   不要把錢放在你褲子的後袋。

2. It's summer now, I wanna buy some short-sleeved shirts.
   現在是夏天，我想購買一些短袖襯衫。

3. Does it fit? Too tight or too loose?
   是否合身？太緊或太鬆？

4. Your fly is open.
   您的拉鍊沒拉。

5. Grey is not my color.
   灰色不是我的顏色。

6. Do you have this in a size 15?
   你們這件有15號的嗎？

7. All sports shoes are out on display.
   所有的運動鞋都在展示。

服裝、鞋子、配件 14

1. 20 ways to wear a scarf----the title of the book really intrigues me.
   20 種戴圍巾的方法----這本書的書名確實吸引我。

2. What are the latest fashion trends?
   什麼是最新的流行趨勢？

3. Your earrings match this necklace.
   你的耳環和這條項鍊很搭配。

4. Upcoming events: Annual sale!
   近期活動：年度特價！

5. Casual shoes make me feel more comfy.
   休閒鞋讓我感覺更舒服。

說明

comfy是comfortable的縮寫。

服裝、鞋子、配件 15

A Your shoes are so gorgeous. Where did you buy them from? I gotta get a pair for myself.
你的鞋子好漂亮。你從哪裡買的？我得給自己也買一雙。

B The shoes were custom-made. You can't find them anywhere else.
這雙鞋子是定做的。你在其他地方找不到。

A I see. They match your pants, too.
我瞭解。它們和你的褲子很配。

B You know what? You're always a person of good taste! That's why I admire you so much.
你知道嗎？你總是一個品味良好的人！這就是為什麼我這麼欣賞你。

A I am so flattered!
真謝謝你的稱讚！

Chapter 7

交通

Transportation

飛機上

1. Could I get another blanket? I'm a little cold.
   可以再給我一條毯子好嗎？我有點冷。

2. How long will it take before we reach Seattle?
   我們還要多久才能到達西雅圖？

3. Will there be any snack after we take off?
   我們起飛後會不會有任何的零食？

4. Another meal will be served before we land.
   降落前會再一次供餐。

5. I will be back in a moment with your coffee.
   我會馬上帶著你的咖啡回來。

"立刻，馬上" 也可用下列片語或單字：in a minute, just one minute, shortly, very soon, right away.

飛機上 2

1. Can I get something to drink, please?
   可以給我一些東西喝嗎？

2. You need to fill out this immigration form before landing.
   您需要在降落前填寫這張入境表格。

3. May I ask for a specially-prepared dinner? No dairy products, cooked in Asian-style spices, and low in calories.
   可以給我特別準備的晚餐嗎？沒有乳製品，亞洲風味的烹調，而且低卡洛里。

4. The captain is making an announcement.
   機長正在宣佈事情。

5. That flight attendant resembles a movie star a lot.
   那空服員酷似一個電影明星。

飛機上 3

1. I need a bassinet for my baby.
   我需要一個嬰兒床。

2. We have some flight entertainment for you.
   我們有提供一些飛機上的娛樂。

3. You will find the film guide in the pocket in front of you.
   你前面的袋子裡有電影指南。

4. We have fish, chicken, beef, mutton, pork and a vegetarian option.
   我們有魚，雞，牛，羊，豬和素食選項。

5. Have you seen the catalogue for our in-flight shop?
   你有看到我們機上商品的目錄嗎？

6. Would you like to order any duty free goods?
   你想訂購的任何免稅商品？

飛機上 4

A Tell me how to avoid and overcome jet lag.
告訴我如何避免和克服時差。

B Rule No.1: adjust your sleeping schedule.
規則一：調整你的睡眠時間表。

A It's 9 am EST, and 3pm in Paris.
現在是美國東部時間上午9點，巴黎時間下午3點。

B The time zone in Taipei is CST. It's 10pm now.
台北的時區是 CST。現在晚上10點。

說明

> EST = Eastern standard time，美國東岸標準時間。
>
> CST = China standard time，中原標準時間。

A The restroom is occupied.
廁所有人。

飛機上 5

Ⓐ Your items might be confiscated by customs if undeclared.
你帶的東西如果未申報，可能會被海關沒收。

Ⓑ Thanks for reminding me
謝謝你提醒。

Ⓐ Listen! The flight attendant is explaining the usage of a life jacket.
聽！空服員正在解釋救生衣的使用。

Ⓑ I'm all ears!
我正在注意聽！

Ⓐ Ladies and Gentlemen. This is your captain speaking. We're now cruising at 25,000 feet. I'd like to remind you to keep your seat belts fastened.
各位女士先生。我是你們的機長。我們正在25000英尺高度飛行，我想提醒你們將安全帶繫好。

機票

A I'd like to buy a ticket to LA.
我想買張機票到洛杉磯。

B One way or round trip?
單程或來回？

說明

來回票: round-trip ticket 或 return ticket。

回程沒有定期的來回票: open return。

三天後回來: three-day return。

A First class or coach?
頭等艙或經濟艙？

說明

經濟艙英文叫 coach、economy class 或 tourist class。

商務艙叫 business class, 票價高一點。

頭等艙叫 first class, 票價最高。

機票 2

1. Would you like an aisle seat, middle seat or window seat?
   你喜歡靠走道的座位，中間的座位還是靠窗的座位？

2. I need a seat with more leg room.
   我需要一個能舒展腿部空間的座位。

3. I don't want to sit next to an emergency exit.
   我不想坐在緊急出口旁邊的座位。

4. We have put you on the waiting list.
   我們已經把你放在等候名單。

5. Would you like the morning flight, afternoon flight, or red-eye flight?
   你想要早上的航班，下午的航班，或者紅眼航班？

說明

所謂 "紅眼航班" 就是夜間航班，也可叫做 night flight 或 Overnight flight。

機票 3

1. I'd like a seat in the front of the plane.
   我想要一個飛機前排的座位。

如果是飛機後排就說 in the back of the plane.

2. Is this a direct flight?
   這是直航班機？

3. It's a non stop flight to Australia.
   這是直接飛往澳洲的航班。

non 是 "非" 的意思。所以non stop 就是中途不停留轉機的直飛航班。
Refund是退款，因此Non-refundable Ticket：不可退票或更改行程的機票。

4. I want to cancel my reservation to America.
   我想取消預定去美國的機票。

機票 4

1. What is your destination?
   你的目的地是哪裡？

2. When is your departure date?
   機票日期是？

> departure = 出境；arrival = 入境。

3. Are there any discount tickets available?
   是否折扣機票？

4. All tickets for flight S0008 are sold out.
   航班 S0008 所有機票都賣完了。

5. The next flight is also full.
   接下來的航班也客滿。

6. It's more convenient to book airline tickets online.
   網上預定機票更方便。

機場櫃台

A Good morning, ma'am. May I have your boarding ticket and passport, please?

早安，女士。可以給我你的機票和護照嗎？

B Here you are.

給你。

A How many are traveling with you today?

今天有幾個人一起和妳搭機？

B My husband and mother-in-law.

我的丈夫和婆婆。

A Is it just you three traveling today?

只有你們三個人？

B Yes.

是的。

機場櫃台 2

1. Do you have any weapons, firearms, or flammable materials in your luggage?
   你有攜帶任何的武器，槍支，易燃物？

2. Are there any food items that are perishable?
   是否有任何易腐壞的食物？

3. Did anyone you do not know ask you to take any items on the plane for them?
   有沒有妳不認識的人要求你為他們攜帶物品上飛機？

4. Have you had possession of all your luggage since you packed your bags?
   你收拾行李後一直隨身攜帶它們嗎？

5. Have you left your luggage unattended at anytime in the airport?
   在機場時妳是否有離開過這些行李？

機場櫃台 3

A How many bags are you checking in?
你帶了幾個包包？

B Only a hand bag.
只有一個手提包。

A Currently there are no window seats available, is an aisle seat ok for you?
目前沒有靠窗的座位，靠走道的座位可以嗎？

B I would like a seat that is closest to the emergency exit please.
我想要一個最接近緊急出口的座位。

A I am sorry, all seats near the exit have already been taken. We have a seat 2 rows back. Would you like that one?
很抱歉，所有出口附近的座位都已經有人。我們有一個後兩排的座，可以嗎？

海關

Ⓐ May I see your passport, please?
我想看你的護照。

Ⓐ How much luggage do you have?
你有多少行李呢？

Ⓑ A suitcase and a carry on.
一個手提箱和一個隨身包包。

Ⓐ Do you have anything to declare? Any contraband in your luggage?
你有什麼要申報嗎？你的行李裡面有任何違禁品嗎？

Ⓑ I need to declare some items I bought in duty-free shops. No, I am not carrying anything illegal.
我要申報一些在免稅商店買的東西。不，我沒有攜帶任何非法物品。

海關 2

Ⓐ What's the purpose of your visit?
您此行的目的是什麼？

Ⓑ I'm here to see my mom and dad.
看到我的爸爸媽媽。

Ⓐ How long will you be staying within the United States. ?
請問您要在美國待多久？

Ⓑ About three weeks.
大約三個星期。

Ⓐ Where will you be staying during your visit?
訪問期間您住在哪裡？

Ⓑ Pittsburgh, Pennsylvania.
賓州匹茲堡。

海關 3

A Do you need an interpreter?
你是否需要翻譯？

B I think I have a good command of English.
我想我的英語能力很好。

A Have you ever been here before?
你有沒有來過這裡？

B I stayed here with a business group in 2012.
我2012年和一個商業團來過這裡。

A Could you open this suitcase for me?
可以打開這個箱子讓我看嗎？

B No problem.
沒問題。

轉機

1. I'm going to stopover at New York.
   我將停留紐約轉機。

2. Could you please reroute me through
   (via) San Francisco?
   請您讓我經由舊金山轉機好嗎？

> through也可改成via，兩者都是 "藉由"。

3. Excuse me, can you tell me where to
   transfer?
   對不起，你能告訴我在哪裡轉機？

4. Should I reserve a connecting flight?
   我是否應該預定連接航班 (也就是轉機)？

5. If I have a layover more than seven
   hours, I'd like to stay overnight.
   如果我的短暫停留超過7個小時，我想留
   下來過夜。

交通

1. Alex commutes to work by train.
   亞歷克斯乘坐火車通勤上下班。

2. In winter, the roads tend to become icy
   and slippery.
   在冬季，道路會變得結冰又滑。

3. They offer valet parking service.
   他們提供代客泊車服務。

4. How much should I tip the chauffeur?
   我應該付多少小費給司機？

5. Did you spot any ticket machine around?
   你有發現周圍有任何售票機嗎？

6. I am wondering who owns that limo?
   我想知道誰擁有那輛加長型豪華轎車？

7. Oops. I'm low on gas.
   哎呀。車快沒油。

交通 2

1. Don't make a u-turn here.
   這裡不可迴轉。

2. Turn the right turn signal on.
   打開右轉方向燈。

3. Look in the right side mirror.
   查看右側照後鏡。

4. Make a safe right turn.
   做出安全右轉。

5. You just ran through a red light! You
   will be fined!
   你剛才闖紅燈了！你會被罰款！

6. Don't exceed the speed limit.
   不要超速。

7. Unleaded, fill it up. How much do I
   owe you?
   無鉛汽油，加滿。多少錢？

交通 3

1. San Francisco is well known for its cable cars.
   舊金山的纜車很有名。

2. I'll be there at 10, unless the train is late.
   我10點會到那裡，除非火車晚點。

3. What's the phone number of the car rental company?
   租車公司的電話號碼是？

4. Did you see the "dead end" sign? Turn around!
   你看到"此路不通"的號誌嗎？回頭！

5. One way do not enter.
   單行道請勿進入。

6. While riding public transport, it's polite to keep our voices down.
   在公車或任何大眾運輸工具上，降低音量是禮貌。

7. We should rent a roomy van.
   我們應該租一輛寬敞的廂型車。

交通 4

A This is a traffic check. Please pull over and turn off your engine. May I see some ID?
這是路邊臨檢。請靠邊停車並關閉引擎。可以讓我看你的證件？

B Sir, what's wrong?
警察先生，有什麼問題嗎？

A Just a routine job.
只是例行工作。

A I want to buy a boat ticket.
我想買船票。

B Please wait in the line.
請排隊。

說明

這句也可說 Please line up here. Line up = queue up 都是排隊。

交通 5

1. Let's hail a cab.
   讓我們招輛計程車。

2. I got a flat tire. But I don't have a spare tire. I need someone to pump up my tire.
   我有 個輪胎沒氣了。但我沒有備胎。我需要有人幫我的輪胎打氣。

3. During rush hour, most of the seats are taken.
   在尖峰期，大部分座位都有人坐。

4. Many guests embarked on a cruise boat.
   許多嘉賓登上了一條遊船。

> embark用在登上交通工具 (飛機、車輛或船舶)。
> 如果是離開交通工具，就用disembark。

交通狀況

1. We're stuck in a traffic jam. You can start without us.
   我們遇上塞車。你們可以先開始。

2. What's the traffic condition near the museum?
   博物館附近的交通狀況如何？

3. There's road construction, so we have to make a detour. We'll pick you up first, and then we'll go get Shirley.
   道路施工，所以我們要繞道。我們先去接你，然後去接雪莉。

4. The road is closed due to the blizzard.
   由於暴風雪道路封閉。

5. The road is bumpy. It makes her nauseous.
   路很顛簸。這讓她噁心不適。

6. The smooth traffic gives us a good mood.
   交通順暢給我們一個好心情。

交通號誌

Ⓐ Hey! You ran through the stop sign.
嘿！你闖過了停車的標誌。

Ⓑ Oops! I didn't notice.
哎呀！我沒有注意到。

Ⓐ Watch out. There's a road construction sign.
當心。那裡有一個道路施工標誌。

Ⓑ I saw that. You're making me nervous.
我看到了。你讓我很緊張。

Ⓐ We're near schools now. You'd better slow down, don't honk.
我們現在在學校附近。你最好減速，不要按喇叭。

Ⓑ I know. I always follow traffic rules.
我知道。我始終遵守交通規則。

公車

A Does this bus go to Disneyland?
這公車去迪斯尼樂園？

B No, you have to transfer to #563 at Harbor Boulevard.
不，你必須在港口大道轉563號公車。

A How much is the fare?
票價多少？

B 2 dollars for one ride, 10 dollars for a one day pass.
一趟2塊錢，一日通行證10塊錢。

A Got it! When will the bus come?
明白了！公車何時來？

B Here's your timetable. Please show the driver your bus pass when boarding.
時間表給你。上車時請向司機出示車票。

火車站

A Where should I get on the train to Tainan?

我應該在哪裡搭去台南的火車？

B Platform number 2.

二號月台。

A How often do the trains come?

每隔多久一班車？

B About every 40 minutes.

大約每 40 分鐘。

A How much is the fare?

票價多少？

B 50.

50 元。

A I appreciate your help.

感謝你的幫助。

計程車

Ⓐ Can I get a taxi?
可以幫我叫計程車？

Ⓑ What is your destination?
你的目的地？

Ⓐ I'm headed to Liberty Square.
我要去自由廣場。

Ⓑ When should the taxi pick you up?
什麼時候去接你？

Ⓐ The sooner the better.
越早越好。

Ⓑ Do you need a round trip ride?
你需要來回嗎？

Ⓐ That won't be necessary.
不必要。

計程車 2

Ⓐ Where are you going?
你去哪兒？

Ⓑ Superstar Mall.
巨星購物中心。

Ⓐ I think there are two in Taipei. Which one are you going to?
在台北有兩個巨星購物中心。你要哪一個？

Ⓑ The one downtown. Hopefully the traffic is not bad.
市中心那個。希望交通狀況不差。

Ⓐ It shouldn't take long. Probably about 20 minutes. Is this your first time in Taipei?
應該用不了多長時間。大概20分鐘左右。這是你第一次來台北？

Ⓑ No. I've been here many times.
不，我來過很多次。

考駕照

A You look upset, what's wrong?
你看起來很困擾，有什麼不對嗎？

B Nothing. I'm just a little nervous.
沒什麼。我只是有點緊張。

A What are you nervous about?
緊張什麼？

B I will have a road test tomorrow.
明天要路上駕駛測試。

A Don't worry. Everything's gonna be fine.
不要擔心。一切都會 OK 的。

B I hope so.
我希望如此。

考駕照 2

A Did you win the lottery or something? You look so happy!

你中了樂透還是怎麼了？你看起來很高興！

B I just passed the road test after failing two times.

我剛通過路考，在經歷兩次失敗後。

A Glad to hear that. Soon you will have a driver's license. Now I am busy studying. Hopefully, I will pass the written test.

很高興聽到這個消息。很快你就會有駕駛執照。我正忙於讀書。希望我會通過筆試。

B Don't worry! You're going to do just fine.

別擔心！你會做得很好。

A Thank you for your encouragement.

感謝你的鼓勵。

學習駕照

Ⓐ I just got my driver's permit not long ago.

我不久前剛拿到我的學習駕照。

說明

> 很多國家規定取得正式駕照前，須有"學習
> 許可"或"學習駕照"(driver's permit 或
> learner's permit)。

Ⓑ Watch out for all the traffic signs when you're driving!

當你開車時，注意所有的交通標誌！

Ⓐ Certainly! The speed limit is 50 mph. I am driving only 45 mph.

當然！限速是 50 英里每小時。我的速度只有45英里每小時。

說明

> mph就是 miles per hour的縮寫，代表速度單
> 位: 英里／小時。

找人搭載

A My car won't start. I need someone to drive me to work.

我的車將無法發動。我需要有人開車送我去上班。

B I can take you. What's your location?

我可以帶你。您的位置在哪？

A I know I can count on you. I am in front of the police station.

我就知道我可以依靠你。我在派出所前面。

A Do you need me to pick you up after work also?

你下班後也需要我接你嗎？

B Yes, if it's not too much trouble.

是的，如果不會太麻煩。

A Not at all. I'll be there shortly.

一點也不。我會很快到那裡。

修車

1. My car broke down. I need a tow truck.
   我的車壞了。我需要一台拖車。

2. I have a dent on my car and it's rusty.
   我的車有一個凹痕，它生鏽了。

3. Will my car insurance cover the repairs?
   我的汽車保險涵蓋修理費用？

4. I got an estimate and it's 2,500 bucks.
   我得到一個估價，得花2500美元。

5. Please bring all of your registration papers.
   請攜帶你所有的註冊文件。

6. My car won't be fixed until Friday. So tomorrow I will walk to my office.
   我的車週五不會修好。所以明天我將走路去辦公室。

車發不動

A My car won't start.
我車發不動。

B What's wrong?
哪裡有問題嗎？

A I think it's out of gas.
我想是沒油了。

B Do you know where the nearest gas station is?
你知道最近的加油站在哪嗎？

A I have no idea.
我不知道。

B Do you need someone to tow your car?
需要有人幫你拖吊嗎？

A I'm afraid so.
恐怕是如此。

租車

A Hi. I would like to rent a car.
你好。我想租一輛車。

B Because you didn't make a reservation, so your options are limited.
因為你沒有預約，所以你的選擇是有限的。

A That's ok. I only want a sedan.
沒關係。我只想要一輛轎車。

B We have one blue sedan available. How long will you be renting this car?
我們有一輛藍色轎車可供您使用。請問您要租多久？

A Just two days.
只需兩天。

B The total will be NT\$4,200. Can I see your driver's license?
總金額是新台幣 4,200 元。我能看你的駕照嗎？

通行證

A I would like to get a day pass for Metro.

我想買地鐵一日票。

B If you travel a lot, maybe you should consider getting a weekly or monthly pass. It'll save you money.

如果你常坐地鐵旅遊，也許你應該考慮買一張週票或月票。它可以節省你的錢。

說明

pass是捷運票或通行證，day pass可一日不限次數搭乘，weekly pass 與 monthly pass則是一周內或一月內不限次數搭乘。

A Actually, I don't travel that much. I think a day pass would be fine for me. Anyway, thanks for your suggestion.

事實上，我沒那麼常旅行。我想買一日票就好。無論如何，感謝您的建議。

搭便車

A Where are you heading?
你往哪個方向？

B I'm heading north to Keelung.
朝北往基隆。

A Can you give me a ride?
可以載我一程嗎？

B Come on in.
進來吧。

A Please drop me off near the post office.
請在郵局附近放我下車。

B OK!
好的！

搭便車 2

Ⓐ Where are you going?
你們去哪兒？

Ⓑ We're going to the Miramar.
我們要去美麗華。

Ⓐ Terrific! I was about to go there. Can I tag along with you guys?
太棒了！我正要去那裡。我可以跟你們去嗎？

Ⓑ But we will go to 5th avenue first to get a car wash. It might take 30 minutes. Are you willing to wait?
但我們會先去第五大道洗車。這可能需要30分鐘。你是否願意等嗎？

Ⓐ Forget it! I will take the metro.
算了吧！我坐捷運。

說明

tag along with someone就是尾隨某人。

搭便車 3

A I just missed the last bus. Can you give me a lift home?

我剛錯過了末班公車。你能載我回家嗎？

說明

> give me a lift和 give me a ride 一樣，是 "載 我一程" 的意思。

B Hop in!

跳上車吧！

說明

> Hop in也可改成 Get in the car 或Jump in the car。

A I owe you one.

我欠你一個人情。

B You can buy me a cup of coffee tomorrow.

你明天可以買一杯咖啡請我。

地理位置

1. Japan is northeast of Taiwan.
   日本在台灣東北方。

2. Canada is north of the USA.
   加拿大在美國北方。

3. I'm a standing on a corner in western Texas.
   我站在德州西部的一個角落。

4. Alaska is near the North Pole.
   阿拉斯加靠近北極。

5. I want to enjoy my vacation on a tropical island.
   我想在一個熱帶島嶼享受我的假期。

6. Taipei is the capital of Taiwan.
   台北是台灣的首都。

7. Wanna visit Germany and the adjacent countries?
   想去德國和鄰近國家旅行？

問路

Ⓐ Is there a grocery store near here?
這附近有雜貨店嗎？

Ⓑ Yes, there's one on Forbes Avenue.
是的，在福布斯大道上有一個。

Ⓐ How can I get there? Is it within walking distance?
我要怎麼去？走路能到嗎？

Ⓑ Yes, it's 15 minutes' walk. Go down this street for two more blocks, turn left, you will see a grocery store on your right.
是的，走路十五分鐘。沿著這條街走兩個街區，左轉，你會看到在你的右邊有一間雜貨店。

說明

block就是 "區塊"，也可當作 "街區"（上下左右四條路圍成的正方形）。所以go two more blocks也就是再走兩條街。

問路 2

Ⓐ Do you know how to get to Apple theater?

你知道如何去蘋果戲院？

Ⓑ It's kind of far from here. Go straight down this road.

離這裡有點遠。這條路直走

Ⓐ OK, I've got it.

我知道。

Ⓑ When you get to the third light, turn right, then go two more blocks. It's kind of complex. Do you need me to tell you again?

當你到了第三個紅綠燈處，右轉，然後走兩個街區。這有點複雜，你需要我再說一次嗎？

Ⓐ You don't have to tell me again. Thanks.

你不用再說一次，謝謝。

Ⓑ Don't mention it.

不用提 (不用說謝謝)。

問路 3

1. I need to go to the MRT station. Can someone give me directions?
   我需要去地鐵捷運站。有人可以給我一個方向？

2. Take a right at the next traffic light.
   在下一個紅綠燈右轉。

3. After you pass the hospital, take a left.
   經過醫院後，向左轉。

4. Turn left at the end of the hallway.
   在走道盡頭左轉。

5. Keep going for another 300 meters.
   繼續走300公尺。

6. It's one mile straight ahead of you.
   在你前方1英里。

7. I have no idea. I'm not from around here.
   我不知道。我不是這裡人。

問路 4

1. Can you point me to the nearest bus stop?
   你可以指引我到最近的公車站牌？

2. What is the best way to get to the cinema?
   去電影院的最佳路徑是什麼？

3. Where's the closest convenience store?
   最近的便利商店在哪？

4. The museum is a red building opposite the fire station.
   博物館是消防局對面的紅色建築物。

5. At the end of the street you will see a roundabout.
   在街的盡頭，你會看到一個圓環。

6. Cross this street, it's between baker's store and florist.
   穿過這條街，它在麵包店和花店之間。

7. It's about a 50-minute bus ride.
   搭公車約50分鐘。

警笛

A Did you hear the siren? Can you tell it's an ambulance or a fire truck?

你聽到警笛聲嗎？你可以分辨它是救護車或消防車？

說明

> tell 原本是 "說"。但有時的意思是 "分辨"。

B I think they all sound the same. Maybe it's a squad car.

我覺得它們的聲音聽起來都一樣。也可能是警車。

A Don't know what's going on. The sound of a siren always makes me nervous.

不知道發生甚麼事。警笛的聲音總是讓我很緊張。

B I do hope nothing serious happened.

我希望沒什麼嚴重的事發生。

MEMO

Chapter 8

買賣

Trade

購物

1. We offer 24/7/365 customer support.
   我們提供全年無休的客戶服務。

2. Buy one get one free.
   買一送一。

3. Two for 399!
   兩個399！

4. He gave the waiter a dollar as a tip.
   他給侍者　美元作為小費。

5. Keep the change.
   不用找了。

說明

change可當作零錢，因此Keep the change表
示請對方把零錢自己留著。

購物 2

A Are you looking for anything in particular?
你有特別找什麼嗎？

B I'm shopping for a dining table. Do you have any suggestions?
我想買餐桌。你有什麼建議嗎？

A Tina likes to go window shopping.
蒂娜喜歡去逛街。

B Maybe she can find some good deals.
也許她可以找到一些不錯的交易。

A Look at all these shoes you bought. You don't wear them that often. Why waste money?
看看你買的這些鞋子。你又不常穿它們。為什麼要浪費錢？

B I like to collect shoes.
我喜歡收集鞋子。

打折

Ⓐ How much is that raincoat?
雨衣價格是多少？

Ⓑ 299.

Ⓐ May I have a discount?
我可以有折扣嗎？

Ⓑ Sorry, it's a fixed price item.
對不起，這是一個固定價格的項目。

說明

這句也可說No bargain---不可討價還價。

Ⓐ How about the boots? Can you give me 10% off?
靴子呢？你可以給我10%優惠嗎？

說明

10%優惠也就是中文"打九折"。同理，15% off也就是"打八五折"。

付款方式

1. Here's the down payment. I will remit the remaining part to you afterwards.
   這裡是訂金。剩餘的部分我以後匯給你。

2. He deposits his paycheck every Friday.
   他每星期五存入他的薪水支票。

3. They promised to pay a deposit of 15%.
   他們承諾支付15％的訂金。

4. The boy returned the bottle and got his five-cent deposit back.
   男孩退回了空瓶，並拿回五美分的押金。

5. I paid for the furniture in 6 monthly installments.
   我用6個月分期付款買這家具。

6. Do you want to pay by cash or credit card?
   你想用現金或信用卡支付？

信用卡

Ⓐ There's a problem with my credit card.
我的信用卡出現一個問題。

Ⓑ Please tell me what the problem is.
請告訴我是什麼問題。

Ⓐ I was charged for something I didn't buy.
帳單出現我沒買的東西。

Ⓑ Can you tell me your card number, 3-digit security code and expiration date?
你能告訴我你的卡號，3位數的授權碼和有效日期嗎？

Ⓐ Do I need to tell you my billing address?
我需要告訴你我的帳單地址嗎？

Ⓑ That won't be necessary, Ma'am. Did you add an additional cardholder last month?
這是不必要的，女士。你上個月加了一個副卡持卡人？

退貨

A Can I help you?
有甚麼可以為你服務嗎？

B Yes, I bought these shoes last month, but they started falling apart.I want my money back.
上個月我買了這雙鞋子，現在已經裂開了，我想拿回我的錢。

A Do you have the sales receipt?
是否有收據？

B No, I don't.
沒有

A I am sorry, according to our refund & exchange policy, we have to have the receipt. Besides, the refund period is one week. It's too late now.
很抱歉，根據我們的退換貨政策，我們必須要有收據。其次，退貨期間是一星期，現在已經太晚。

退貨 2

A I'd like to return this dishwasher.
這個洗碗機我想退貨。

B Is there something wrong with it?
有什麼問題嗎？

A It didn't work well for me. Besides, it's too loud and it took up too much space.
它讓我覺得不好用。此外，它的聲音太大了，它也佔用了太多空間。

B You've got the receipt with you?
你帶了收據嗎？

A Here you go.
在這裡。

B Are you considering buying other types of dishwashers?
您是否考慮購買其他類型的洗碗機？

換錢

A Do you exchange foreign currency?
你們兌換外幣？

B Yes, we do.
是的，我們有。

A I want to change 50 dollars for Euros.
What is the exchange rate?
我想將50美元換成歐元。匯率是多少？

B It's about one dollar to 0.95 Euros.
大約一每元兌換0.95歐元。

A Do you charge commission?
你們收取佣金？

B We charge 2%.
我們收取2％。

 說明

Won：韓圜，Yen：日圓，RMB：人民幣，
British pound：英鎊。

換錢 2

Ⓐ Could you change some money for me?
你能換些錢給我嗎？

Ⓑ I'll be glad to.
我很樂意。

Ⓐ Please break this 20 dollar bill into one 10 and two 5's.
請將這張 20 美元的鈔票換成一張 10 元和兩張 5 元。

Ⓑ No problem. What else can I do for you?
沒問題。我還能為你做點什麼？

Ⓐ Can I cash my traveler's checks here?
我可以兌現我的旅行支票嗎？

Ⓑ My pleasure!
是我的榮幸！

Ⓐ I really appreciate it
我真的很感激。

結束營業

A I just heard Molly bookstore is going out of business.
我剛才聽到茉莉書店即將歇業。

B Are you kidding?
你在開玩笑吧？

A I am serious.
我是認真的。

B Your friend Jenny works there, right?
你的朋友珍妮在那裡工作，對吧？

A She just started to work there about three months ago.
她大約三個月前才開始在那上班。

B Did she know what's going on?
她知道發生甚麼事嗎？

商店或賣場

A Good evening, sir.
先生晚安。

B I want a bar of chocolate.
給我一條巧克力棒。

A There you go.
在這裏。

B Thanks a lot!
多謝！

A Have a nice day!
祝你有個美好的一天！

B You too.
你也是。

說明

Have a nice day! 通常是商店店員結完帳時對顧客說的話，也可用 Have a good one 取代。

逛超市

Ⓐ Do you need any help finding anything?
你需要幫忙尋找什麼嗎？

Ⓑ Where is the fruit section?
水果區在哪？

Ⓐ They are over on aisle F.
他們在 F 走道上.

Ⓑ Can you point me to the toys area?
你能指出玩具區在哪？

Ⓐ Please take the escalator to the 2nd
floor, then look to your left.
請乘手扶梯到二樓，再看你的左邊。

Ⓑ Do you sell cameras here?
你這裡賣相機嗎？

逛賣場

Ⓐ Where are the shopping carts?
購物推車在哪？

Ⓑ There are no shopping carts available right now. Do you want a shopping basket?
現在沒有推車可用。購物籃好嗎？

Ⓐ Is there any item on sale?
有沒有任何商品特價？

Ⓑ Please look in this flyer, or check with the produce person over there. He will be more than happy to help you.
請看這個傳單，或詢問那邊的服務人員。
他會很樂意為您服務。

produce person就是賣場服務人員，負責將商品上架，或向顧客介紹產品等。

銀行

1. This is your ATM card. Please don't forget your pin.
   這是你的提款卡。請不要忘記你的密碼。

2. Be careful of fraud when you transfer money to another person's account.
   當你轉帳到別人的帳戶時，小心詐騙。

3. What is today's interest rate?
   今天的利率是多少？

4. I have some coins I need to change.
   我有一些硬幣，我需要換錢。

5. I need a safety deposit box.
   我需要一個保險箱。

6. With a smart phone or any kind of mobile device, you can use our mobile banking services.
   用智慧手機或任何一種行動裝置，您就可以使用我們的行動銀行服務。

網路銀行

A Do you offer internet banking? Can you explain to me how it works?

你們提供網路銀行服務？你能向我解釋它是如何運作的？

B Absolutely, sir. We do offer internet banking. Internet Banking is available whenever you're online. So you can do your banking whenever and wherever you want.

當然，先生。我們提供網路銀行。當您上網時，網路銀行可隨時提供服務。所以，無論何時何地，你都可以進行銀行交易。

A It sounds perfect. I work the night shift. It's difficult for me to go to the bank during normal business hours.

這聽起來很完美的。我上夜班，很難在正常營業時間去銀行。

買電腦

A I wanna buy a computer. Do you have any recommendations?"
我想買一台電腦。你有什麼建議？

B Why do you need a computer?
為什麼你需要一台電腦？

A Internet surfing mainly.
上網為主。

B You want a laptop or a PC?
你想要筆記型或桌上型電腦？

A I think a laptop is more convenient for me.
我認為筆記型電腦對我來說更方便。

B This is the best one to fit your needs.
這台最能滿足您的需求。

買外套

A Is this coat too big for me?
這外套對我來說是否太大？

B It's a perfect fit.
完美合身。

A Alright. I will take it.
好的。我買這件。

B Cash or charge?
現金或刷卡？

A I'll charge it.
刷卡。

B Please sign here.
請在這裡簽名

A I want a receipt.
我要一張收據。

賣房子

A Why do you smile so much?
你為什麼充滿笑容？

B I just successfully sold my house!
我剛成功賣出我的房子！

A I am so happy for you.
我真為你高興。

B I did it all on my own, without a middleman. It took me only two weeks. It's quicker than I expected.
這一切我自己辦到的，沒有靠中間人。我只有花兩個星期。這比我預期的更快。

A You're really something!
你真了不起！

B Thanks for your compliment.
謝謝你的誇獎。

洗碗機

A Ma'am. You got a minute? Would you like to take a look at our dishwasher? Please have a seat and let me show you how to operate it.

夫人。可以給我一分鐘嗎？你想不想看看我們的洗碗機？請坐，讓我展示如何操作。

B Ok.

好吧。

A All you have to do is to press the blue button. Just that simple!

你所有要做的就是按下藍色按鈕。就這麼簡單！

B Looks like It's pretty convenient and easy to use! Can I have a copy of your brochure?

看起來這是很方便和易於使用的！可以給我一份介紹手冊？

有線電視

A I would like to order cable.
我想訂有線電視。

B What kind of package do you prefer?
你喜歡什麼樣的頻道組合？

A Except the basic channels, I also want all the music and movie channels.
除了基本的頻道，我也想要所有的音樂和電影頻道。

B How about news and sports?
新聞和體育呢？

A I am not interested in those.
我對那些不感興趣。

A OK. If you change your mind later, you can add or remove channels.
好的。如果您以後改變主意，你可以增加或刪除頻道。

剪髮

A I need to get a haircut, can I schedule an appointment?
我要理髮，可以預約嗎？

B You have a particular day in mind?
你有計畫哪個特定的日子？

A Is next Monday OK?
下週一好不好？

B Let me check my book. Is 3pm a good time for you?
讓我看看我的本子。下午3點好嗎？

A That's perfect! I will bring my own shampoo. See you then.
完美！我會帶我自己的洗髮精。到時候見。

剪髮 2

1. I want to try something new today. I want a different hair style.
   我今天想嘗試新的東西。我想要一個不同的髮型。

2. Can you make my hair short? Make it about 5 inches long.
   你能不能簡短我的頭髮？讓它大約5英寸長。

3. I would like to perm my hair now, a curly perm.
   我現在想燙髮，燙捲髮。

4. I am thinking about coloring my hair brown.
   我想將我的頭髮染成棕色。

5. I want to book a manicure and a pedicure.
   我要預訂修指甲和修腳。

剪髮 3

1. I want to dye my hair purple.
   我想把我的頭髮染成紫色。

2. Please trim my hair a little.
   請修剪一點我的頭髮。

3. I told the hair stylist to have my hair straightened.
   我告訴髮型師把我的頭髮拉直。

4. I still don't understand the difference between a barber shop and a hair salon.
   我還是不明白一個理髮店和美髮沙龍之間的差異。

5. Just cut a little above the ears.
   稍微剪短到耳朵上方。

6. Please make my hair thinner. Does it look good to get layers in my hair?
   請打薄我的頭髮。我如果頭髮有層次好看嗎？

Chapter 9

工作

Work

工作

1. I got a tight schedule this week.
   這週我的時間表很緊湊。

2. You might finish your work ahead of schedule.
   您可能會進度超前完成工作。

3. This project is behind schedule by 20 days.
   本專案落後進度20天。

4. Let's call it a day.
   讓我們收工。

5. What held you up this morning?
   今天上午你為何遲到？

6. It's your turn to say something.
   輪到你發言。

7. Tell us more about your previous work experience.
   告訴我們更多關於你之前的工作經驗。

工作 2

I try to keep in mind the following things at my workplace.

在我的工作場所，我試圖記住下面這些事情。

1. Always have a positive attitude.

   永遠抱持一個積極的態度。

2. Always hope for the best and prepare for the worst.

   永遠做最好的期望和為可能發生的最壞情況做準備。

3. Always seek professional help when I need it.

   當我需要時，永遠尋求專業人士的協助。

4. Always stay aloof from coworkers that are a bad influence.

   永遠遠離會帶來不好影響的同事。

說明

stay aloof from 等於 stay away from。

工作 3

1. I have read all the complaint letters from customers.
   我已經讀完所有客戶的抱怨信件。

2. The copy machine is jammed again.
   影印機又卡住了。

3. We have run out of pencils and paper.
   我們已經用完了鉛筆和紙。

4. Welcome aboard. I'm Brian.
   歡迎加入。我是布萊恩。

5. These two departments must learn to coexist.
   這兩個部門必須學習共存。

說明

通常co有 "共同" 的意思，例如：coexist 共同存在，coworker同事，cofounder共同創辦人。

工作 4

1. I will be there. You can take my word for it.
   我會在那裡。你可以相信我的話。

2. I like to have a word with you. Please come to my office.
   我有話想跟你說。請來我的辦公室。

3. You don't push the button. It doesn't work that way.
   您不該按下按鈕。這樣行不通的。

4. Can he deal with a heavy workload?
   他能應付繁重的工作？

5. I am in charge of the local branch of BCC bank.
   我負責 BCC 銀行的本地分行。

6. It's the 3rd time this month she took a leave of absence.
   這是這一個月她第三次請假。

工作 5

1. Nobody likes an employee with a rowdy behavior.
   沒有人喜歡行為粗魯的員工。

2. I like to put everything in order.
   我喜歡讓一切井然有序。

3. It's not personal. Don't take it to heart.
   這不是針對個人的。不要把它放在心上。

4. I must learn more about how to handle tough situations.
   我必須學習更多如何處理困難狀況。

5. Who is the former CEO of Intel?
   誰是英特爾的前任執行長？

說明

CEO = chief executive officer。
CFO = chief financial officer 財務長。
CIO = chief information officer 資訊長。

工作 6

1. There's a job opening at my company. I can arrange an interview next week if you want.
   我的公司有一個職缺。如果你想，我下週可安排一個面試。

2. I will continue to do my best and contribute to the company.
   我會繼續盡我所能，有助於公司。

3. How I wish you were my boss.
   我多麼希望你是我的老闆。

說明

使用不可能成真的假設語氣時，用過去式取代現在式。

例句 1：Wish you were here.

希望你在這裡。（但你明明不在這裡。）

例句 2：If I were a bird...

如果我是一隻鳥……（不可能成真。）

工作 7

1. Your cooperation is very much appreciated.
   非常感謝您的合作。

2. I am so happy to make a deal with you.
   我很樂意與您達成協議。

3. I finally figured it out.
   我終於把它搞懂了。

4. We can work it out.
   我們可以解決這個問題。

5. Do you want me to show you around?
   你要我帶你四處看看？

6. We have to share the printer with other departments.
   我們必須與其他部門分享影印機。

7. That's how it works.
   它就是如此運作的。

工作 8

1. Any time, pal. You know where I am.
   任何時候都可以找我，夥伴。你知道我在哪裡。

2. It's not that difficult to get along with your coworkers.
   和你的同事好好相處並沒那麼困難。

3. You made a typo, just cross it out.
   您打了一個錯字，刪掉就好。

4. I am having a problem finding the right documents. I need your assistance.
   我找不到正確的文件。我需要你的幫助。

5. Please turn the music down. It's still working time.
   請把音樂關小聲。現在還是上班時間。

---

turn the music up 將音樂開大聲。

工作 9

A What do you like most about your job?

你最喜歡你工作的哪個部分？

B It's a good paying job with flexible working hours.

Besides, the coworkers are friendly.

它是一個薪水不錯的工作，工時有彈性，同事都很友善。

A Do you consider yourself a good employee?

你認為自己是個好員工嗎？

B I am very committed to my work.

我非常投入我的工作。

說明

coworker 也可用 colleague，兩者都是"同事"。

工作時間

A I prefer the morning shift to the evening shift.
我喜歡早班勝於晚班。

B Me too, I also feel more energetic in the daytime.
我也是，我也覺得白天比較精力充沛。

A What time do you usually leave the office?
你一般什麼時間離開辦公室？

B Around 5 PM.
下午5點左右。

A Let us meet as soon as your shift ends.
你輪完班後我們立刻見面。

B OK, don't be late.
不要遲到。

公司福利

A What are the benefits that your company provides?
貴公司提供那些福利？

B Insurance, paid vacation. The dress code allows us to wear casual clothes.
保險，帶薪休假。公司的服裝規定准許我們上班著休閒服裝。

A How about promotion opportunities?
升遷的機會如何？

B I just received a nice job promotion. They will also give me a salary increase starting next month.
我剛剛才升官。他們下月開始也要幫我加薪。

A Do you work long hours?
你工作時間長嗎？

B It depends.
這要看情況。

請人幫忙

A I need to have my car repaired by noon. Please give me a hand.
中午前我需要將我的車修好。請幫我。

B But I don't see our mechanic around. He might be in the basement.
但我沒看到我們的技師在附近。他可能在地下室。

A Are you a morning person?
你是一個早起的人？

B No, I sleep pretty late.
不，我睡得很晚。

A You sure you can do this?
你確定你能做到？

B No sweat.
沒問題。

找東西

Ⓐ I couldn't find my files, usually they are in my filing cabinet. Did you see them?

我找不到我的文件，通常他們是在我的文件櫃。你看到了嗎？

Ⓑ No. Did you look on the shelf?

沒看到。你有看過是否在架上？

Ⓐ Which shelf?

哪個架子？

Ⓑ Try the top one.

頂端那個。

Ⓐ Not there.

不在那裏。

Ⓑ Check in the desk middle drawer or the bottom drawer.

檢查辦公桌中間或底部的抽屜。

感謝與道歉

A Thanks for your information.
謝謝妳提供的資訊。

B Sure thing!
不客氣。

A I appreciate your help.
感謝妳的幫助。

B My pleasure.
不客氣。

A I'm so sorry.
我真的很抱歉。

B No Problem!
沒關係。

稱讚對方的成就

A I've finished reading your report.
我已讀完你的報告。

B How do you feel about it?
你覺得如何？

A You've done a wonderful job.
你完成了一個很棒的工作。

B I'm not so sure.
我沒那麼確定。

A You're really modest.
你真是謙虛。

B I'm glad you like it.
很高興你喜歡。

A You know what? You have always been a great employee.
你知道嗎？你一直是一個很好的員工。

名片

Ⓐ Can I get your contact information?
可以給我您的聯絡方式？

Ⓑ My contact information is on my business card. Let me give you one. May I have yours?
我的聯絡方式在我的名片上面。讓我給你一張。可以給我你的嗎？

Ⓐ Certainly! What is the best way to contact you?
當然可以！什麼是與您聯繫的最佳方式？

Ⓑ You can reach me at my cell phone number or email address. You can also send text messages to me.
您可以透過手機或電子郵件聯絡我。您也可以發簡訊給我。

"發簡訊給我" 也可用text me較為簡單。

當志工

Ⓐ I think my life is pretty boring.
我覺得我的生活很無聊。

Ⓑ Why do you say so?
你為什麼這麼說？

Ⓐ I wake up at 6 am every morning, I leave for work at 7, work until 6pm, then I go home.
我每天早上6點醒來，7點離家去上班，一直工作到下午6點，然後回家。

Ⓑ Perhaps you can try something different.
或許你可以嘗試不同的東西。

Ⓐ What are your suggestions?
你有什麼建議？

Ⓑ For example: working as a volunteer for charitable organizations. Maybe you'll find the meaning of life.
例如：為慈善機構當志工。也許你會發現生命的意義。

詢問對方工作

A Where are you working now?
你現在在哪裡工作？

B I am an engineer in a local company.
我是本地一家公司的工程師。

A That sounds cool. You must be very good at what you do.
這聽起來很酷。你一定很擅長你的工作內容。

B How about you?
那你呢？

A I am a volunteer worker in some schools.
我在一些學校當志工。

B You are such a wonderful person! I believe you have a good work ethic.
你真是一個很棒的人！我相信你有很好的工作道德。

詢問對方工作 2

A What is your occupation?
你從事什麼職業？

B I'm a writer. What sort of job do you have?
我是一個作家。你做什麼樣的工作？

A I am a retired businessman.
我是一名退休商人。

B Really? I used to run a small business selling toys.
真的嗎？我以前經營一個小生意賣玩具。

A That is really interesting.
那真是非常有趣。

B That's why I always have a childlike heart.
這就是為什麼我常保一顆孩童般的心。

詢問對方工作 3

Ⓐ What does his sister do?
他姊姊從事甚麼工作？

Ⓑ She runs a small convenience store.
她經營著一家小便利商店。

Ⓐ Does Cindy work full-time or part-time?
辛蒂全職工作或兼職工作？

Ⓑ She is a full-time nurse. She is also a part-time worker in a library.
她是一名全職護士。也在圖書館兼職工作

Ⓐ What's your line of work?
你的職業是什麼？

Ⓑ I am an amateur photographer.
我是一名業餘攝影師。

amateur是業餘，專業是professional。

詢問對方工作 4

Ⓐ What do you do for a living?
你是做什麼工作的？

Ⓑ I work at the local college teaching French. How about you?
我在本地一所大學教法語。你呢？

Ⓐ I was a chemical engineer, but am currently out of work.
我是一位化學工程師，但目前沒有工作。

Ⓑ Sorry to hear that. Don't worry. I will introduce you to a friend of mine. Maybe he can give you a new job.
很遺憾聽到這個。不要擔心。我將向你介紹我的一個朋友，也許他可以給你一個新的工作。

Ⓐ That sounds great!
這聽起來很棒！

整理辦公室

A Can you help me tidy my office?
你能不能幫我整理我的辦公室？

B What do you want me to do?
你想要我做什麼？

A Make sure all the documents go into the drawer.
確定所有的文件放進抽屜裡。

B How about that paper over there?
那裡的紙張呢？

A Don't throw it away. We should recycle paper to save trees.
不要扔掉。我們應該回收紙來拯救樹木。

B We can also reuse these plastic bags, they are not dirty at all.
我們還可以重複使用這些塑膠袋，它們一點也不髒。

辭職解雇

A I heard that you got laid off from your job.
我聽說你被解雇了我聽說你

說明

解雇除了用 laid off 以外，也可用 fired。

B No, that's not true.
不，這不是真的

A So, what happened?
發生了什麼事？

B I quit my job to go back to school.
我辭掉工作回到學校。

A Good for you!
好樣的！

B Let's keep in touch.
讓我們保持聯繫。

Chapter 10

旅遊休閒

Travel & Leisure

電影

A Let's watch a movie after dinner.
我們晚餐後去看電影。

B Why not? How about Kiwi paradise?
為什麼不呢？看"奇異果天堂"如何？

A Absolutely! What time should we meet at the theatre?
當然可以！我們什麼時候在劇院碰面？

說明

通常cinema專指電影院，而theater除了播放電影，也可能做為戲劇表演的場所。

B Let's meet in front of Starbucks at 4pm.
我們下午4點在星巴克門前見面。

A OK. Don't stand me up.
OK。不要放我鴿子。

電影 2

A I'm so bored, let's go see a movie.
我很無聊，讓我們去看電影。

B I'm with you. What's on these days?
我同意。現在正在上映甚麼電影？

說明

with有和某人在一起的意思，例如：He is with me------他和我在一起。但有時with也可表示"同意"。

A I heard they're playing "Love never fails ".
我聽說正在演"愛永不失敗"。

B Cool! My brother said it's a must see.
酷！我哥哥說，這是一部必看電影。

說明

It's a must.---這是必須的。
A must eat-----必吃美食。

電影 3

1. Titanic is coming out this Saturday.
   這個週六開始上演鐵達尼號。

2. The Rocky series consists of seven movies.
   洛基系列包括七部電影。

3. That horror film really made me scared!
   那恐怖片真讓我害怕！

film和movie都是電影。

4. All the young guys I know love action movies.
   我認識的所有年輕傢伙都喜愛動作片。

5. I want to see machine cops on opening day.
   我希望在首映當天看機器警察。

電影 4

1. Not every girl likes romance movies, for example: me.
   不是每個女孩都喜歡浪漫電影，例如：我。

2. How much do newly released movies cost to rent?
   租新發行影片要多少錢？

3. That comedy film is so hilarious!
   這喜劇電影太好笑了！

4. Every theater is booked out tonight. Please try again tomorrow.
   今晚每個劇院的票都被訂完了。請明天再試。

5. Me and my buddy wanna see The Matrix. When does it start?
   我和我的朋友想看駭客任務。它幾點開始？

比較正統的說法是my friend and I，me and my buddy是年輕人不合乎文法的常用語。

電影 5

1. Some said that movie was really great, but I was so disappointed. As a matter of fact, I walked out of the cinema before it ended .

   有人說那部電影很棒，但我很失望。事實上，我在電影結束之前就走出電影院。

2. I so much enjoy watching all the stunts.

   我很享受觀看所有這些特技。

3. I was holding my breath while watching this scene.

   看著這一幕時我屏住呼吸。

4. Talking about that suspense movie, the ending surprised everybody.

   談到那部懸疑片。結局讓大家都感到驚訝。

5. Of course the main characters in a movie matter most.

   當然，在電影中主角最為重要。

電影 6

1. It's so touching. It moves me to tears.
   它是如此動人。這讓我感動落淚。

2. What are the top 10 drama movies of all time?
   有史以來最佳前10名的戲劇類電影是？

3. Why are you screaming? Don't you know that scary scene is fake?
   你為什麼要尖叫？難道你不知道那可怕的一幕是假的嗎？

4. I think that science fiction movie was overrated by most of the critics.
   我認為那部科幻電影被大部分的影評評價太高了。

說明

overrated是評價大於實質，underrated是實質大於評價。

電影 7

1. "I'll be back" is a very famous movie line.

   "我會回來的"，是一句非常著名的電影台詞。

2. The plots in these 2 films are so similar.

   這2部電影的情節如此相似。

3. Most of the animation movies are entertaining.

   大多數的動畫電影具娛樂性。

4. The captions on DVDs help me understand the films.

   DVD 上的字幕幫助我理解電影。

5. This film is based on a true story.

   這部影片是根據一個真實的故事。

6. Debby wins best actress, Glen wins best supporting actor.

   黛比贏得最佳女主角，格倫贏得最佳男配角。

電視

1. How many TV channels are there in Finland?
   在芬蘭有多少電視頻道？

2. Please help me find the TV remote.
   請幫我找一下電視遙控器。

3. It has been 8 months since its initial run, I can't wait to watch the rerun.
   自從首播到現在已經八個月，我等不及看重播。

4. Speaking of Happy Family series, I never miss an episode.
   說起幸福家庭電視影集，我從未錯過任何一集。

5. I am sort of addicted to that TV series.
   我對那電視影集有點上癮。

說明

sort of等於kind of和somewhat。

借書

Ⓐ I need to check out this book.
我要借這本書。

Ⓑ Do you have a library card?
你有借書證？

Ⓐ No. I don't. Can I apply for one right now?
不，我沒有。我可以申請一張嗎？

Ⓑ Sure! Please fill out the application form
當然！請填寫申請表。

Ⓐ There you go.
寫好了，在這。

Ⓐ Now, please sign your name on the back of the card. Your books are due back one month from today.
請在借書證背面簽上您的名字。書在一個月後到期。

借書 2

1. How much is the late fee per day for books and CDs?
   書籍、CD 每天的滯納金是多少？

2. You have to pay off all the fines before borrowing new books.
   您借新書之前必須還清所有的罰款。

3. These magazines are more than 1 month overdue.
   這些雜誌逾期1個月以上。

4. Library opening hours: Monday to Friday, 8am to 7pm.
   圖書館開放時間：週一至週五，上午8時至晚上七時

5. You may extend the due date of the library books.
   您可以延長借書的截止日期。

6. I must return the books before the grace period ends.
   我必須在寬限期結束前還書。

借書 3

1. Was this book on the shelf?
   這本書在架上？

2. The periodicals section is on the 3rd floor.
   期刊區在三樓。

3. Our policy doesn't allow readers to check out magazines.
   我們的政策不允許讀者借出雜誌。

4. What are the do's and don'ts of this library?
   在這圖書館內何事可做，何事不可做？

5. Printing, scanning and photocopying are for our staff and students only.
   列印，掃描和影印只限我們的員工和學生。

6. Where is the book "Learning Java, 2nd edition" located?
   "學習 Java 第二版" 在哪裡？

書店

A I'm looking for a book called "Food courts in Taipei".
我在找一本書，叫"美食廣場在台北"。

B Please follow me.
請跟我來。

A Can I find the book called "Italian gourmet"?
名為"意大利美食"的書在哪，？

B Oh. I'm afraid it is sold out.
噢。恐怕賣完了。

A Excuse me, what are the top 3 best sellers of 2014?
對不起，什麼是2014年暢銷書的前3名？

B You got me!
你問倒我了！

球賽

A What's your favorite team?
你最喜歡的球隊是？

B I am always a Tigers fan.
我一向是老虎隊的球迷。

A They're playing the Leopards tonight, right?
他們今晚和豹隊比賽，對吧？

B Yeah, I gotta work tonight. So I can only watch the highlights online.
是啊，我今晚必須工作。所以，我只能看線上轉播精華。

A Do you think they'll win the championship this year?
你認為今年他們會贏得冠軍？

B It's highly possible. They have some really good players this year.
這是高度可能的。他們今年有一些非常優秀的球員。

球賽 2

A Do you think Iron Men will beat Supermen tonight?

你認為鐵人隊今晚會打敗超人隊？

B Not a chance.

沒機會。

A You wanna bet?

你想打賭嗎？

B I don't gamble. How much do you usually place a wager on sports?

我不賭博。你通常會在運動賽事下注多少錢？

A 10 bucks.

10塊錢。

B Let me recommend an article for you to read: Gambling is not a good thing to do.

讓我推薦一篇文章供您閱讀：賭博不是一件好事。

球賽 3

1. Supermen have won six games in a row.
   超人隊連續贏了六場比賽。

2. The home team won games 1 and 2, the visiting team won game 3.
   主場球隊贏了第一、二場比賽，客隊贏了第 3 場比賽。

3. Wilt Chamberlain scored 100 points in a single basketball game.
   威爾特張伯倫曾經在單一籃球賽中得了 100 分。

4. Klay Thompson sets an NBA record with 37 points in a quarter.
   克雷·湯普森在一節中得 37 分創 NBA 紀錄。

 說明

quarter 是 1/4，它可以等於兩角五分 (一元的 1/4)，也可以等於一節 (一場比賽的 1/4)。

球賽 4

A Do you like baseball?
你喜歡棒球嗎？

B I like to watch as much as I like to play.
我喜歡看，就像我喜歡玩。

A Do you play often?
你經常玩？

B Every now and then with some friends.
偶而與一些朋友玩。

A What position did you play?
你打什麼位置？

B Normally, a catcher.
通常是捕手。

成語 Every now and then 的意思是"偶而"。

球賽5

1. It's a tied game.
   這場比賽平手。

2. There are 9 innings to a professional baseball game.
   一場職業棒球比賽有9局。

3. He was selected as the best pitcher.
   他被選為最佳投手。

4. The New York Yankees have won 26 World Series titles.
   紐約洋基隊贏得26次世界大賽冠軍。

5. Mike hit a home run in the top of the 7th inning.
   麥克在第7局上半揮出了一個全壘打。

說明

如果是一局的下半就說bottom of the inning。

球賽 6

A Did you go to the basketball game on Saturday?

你上週六有去看籃球比賽？

B No, I couldn't make it. I had to work overtime.

不，我無法趕到。我要加班。

A You missed a really good game.

你錯過了一場非常精彩的比賽。

B What was the score?

比分多少？

A 99-97. The Giants won.

99-97。巨人贏了。

B That was a really close game.

這是一個非常接近的比賽。

球賽 7

1. I shouldn't have invited you to watch this nonsense tennis game. My bad!
   我不該邀請您觀看這個荒謬的網球賽。我的錯！

2. Frank is good at soccer but bad at swimming.
   法蘭克擅長足球，但游泳很糟。

3. Who takes the lead? The Bulls or 76ers?
   誰領先？公牛隊還是76人？

4. The audience applauded like crazy at the end of the game.
   比賽結束時觀眾像瘋了似的鼓掌。

5. We should give a big hand to Dorothy for her wonderful performance.
   我們應該給一個桃樂西一個掌聲為了她的精彩表演。

6. Lions sweep Sharks. It's too good to be true!
   獅子隊橫掃鯊魚隊。這是好得讓人不敢相信！

運動

1. Do you exercise in your spare time?
   你在空閒時間是否鍛煉身體？

2. I fell in love with cycling back in high school.
   高中時代我愛上了騎自行車。

3. Everyone our age needs to do some kind of exercises.
   我們這年紀的每個人都需要做一些運動。

4. Do you like aerobics such as jogging, swimming or something like that?
   你喜歡有氧運動嗎，例如慢跑，游泳之類的事情？

5. By doing so, you can sculpt a firm butt in just 5 moves.
   藉著這樣做，你可以用5個動作雕塑結實的臀部。

6. Have you joined any fitness center?
   你有沒有加入任何健身中心？

健身房

A What should we do today?
我們今天該做什麼？

B I'd like to exercise.
我想運動。

A But it's pretty cold outside.
但外面很冷。

B Let's go to the gym.
讓我們去健身房。

A Good idea, What are you going to do there?
好主意。你去那裏要做什麼？

B Running on a treadmill.
用跑步機。

演奏會

A Are there any special events going on tomorrow?
明天有沒有什麼特別的事件？

B Yes. There will be an outdoor concert in the park tomorrow.
有的。明天公園裡將有一場戶外音樂會。

A All three of you gonna attend the concert?
你們三個都要參加這場音樂會？

B That's right! Do you wanna join us?
是的！你想加入我們嗎？

A Sure, you can count me in. I haven't been to a concert in years.
當然，你們可以把我算在內。我已經幾年沒去過音樂會了。

B Believe me. It's a live performance you don't wanna miss!
相信我。這是一場你不會想錯過的現場表演！

遊樂場

1. There are some slides and swings in the playground.
   在遊樂場上有一些溜滑梯和鞦韆。

2. The twin boys are playing on the seesaw.
   雙胞胎男孩正在玩蹺蹺板。

3. A kindergarten teacher is playing hide and seek with those kids.
   幼稚園老師正在與那些孩子玩捉迷藏。

4. Amy is telling me about her unforgettable roller coaster experience.
   艾美正在告訴我她難忘的雲霄飛車經驗。

說明

> 許多形容詞前面加上un，意思就完全相反。
> 例如：important---重要的。
> unimportant---不重要的。
> 同理，unforgettable---無法忘記的。

嗜好

A What is your major hobby?
你的主要嗜好是什麼？

B Why don't you take a guess?
你為什麼不猜一猜？

A I have a hunch that it's fishing.
我有一種直覺是釣魚。

說明

hunch 和 intuition 都可以當直覺。例句：My intuition says she won't come.----- 我的直覺說她不會來。

B Bingo!
答對了！

A As for me, I like to surf the internet as a pastime.
至於我，我喜歡上網作為一種消遣。

嗜好 2

A What do you do in your spare time?
你空閒時間做些什麼？

B Mostly, going out with my girl friend. How about you? What do you like to do for fun?
大部分時間，和我的女朋友出去走走。你呢？做甚麼事是你的樂趣？

A Reading always brings me great pleasure.
讀書總是帶給我很大的快樂。

B What kind of books do you like to read?
你喜歡看什麼樣的書？

A I'm into a variety of books. Actually, I love biographies of scientists the most.
我喜歡不同種類的書籍。其實，我最愛的是科學家傳記。

照相

A Will you take a picture of us?
可以幫我們照相嗎？

B Sure. How to use it?
當然。如何使用它？

A Just press the red button here.
按下這個紅色按鈕。

B Come a little closer. Move a little to the right.
靠近一點點，往右移一點。

A Do you mean here?
這裡嗎？

B Yes, stay right there. Say cheese!
是的，就是那裏，露出微笑。

 說明

當攝影者要求說 "cheese" 時，表示請被拍照的人露出微笑。

約朋友看演唱會

A Hi, you want to hang out with me and Jackie tonight?
嗨，你今晚想和傑基與我去玩嗎？

B I have chores to do. My mom told me to vacuum the floor in my room.
我有家事要做。我媽媽要我吸我房間的地板。

A How about tomorrow?
明天怎麼樣？

B Tomorrow is fine for me. What's on your mind?
明天我可以。您的想法是什麼？

A I am thinking about maybe we three can go see a concert or something.
我想，也許我們三個人可以去看演唱會什麼的。

B I love that!
我喜歡！

旅遊

A I went on a trip to Europe with my wife last month.
我上個月與我的妻子去歐洲旅遊。

B What? Didn't she talk you out of planning this trip?
什麼？不是她勸你不要計畫這趟旅程嗎？

A On the contrary, she talked me into planning this trip.
相反地，是她勸我計畫這趟旅程的

B Alright, so I heard it wrong.
好吧，所以是我聽錯了。

說明

talk someone out of 和 take someone into 是近來很流行的片語，前者是勸人不要做某事，後者是勸人去做某事。

旅遊 2

1. It's a once in a lifetime journey.
   這是一生只有一次的旅程。

2. Travelling to this city is an eye-opening experience.
   到這個城市旅行是一個讓人大開眼界的經驗。

3. All kids like to go to the amusement park.
   所有小孩都喜歡去遊樂園。

4. You might be able to get some good deals and useful information from a travel agency.
   您也許能從旅行社得到一些不錯的旅程安排和有用的訊息。

5. We all love the Hello Kitty theme café in Malaysia.
   我們都愛馬來西亞的 Hello Kitty 主題餐廳。

說明

dinosaur theme park 恐龍主題公園。

旅遊 3

A Speaking of hygiene, we better bring our own personal items with us when travelling.
說到衛生，旅行時我們最好要帶自己的個人用品。

B I agree with you. I have brought my toothbrush, hairbrush, lipsticks.
我同意你的看法。我帶來了牙刷，梳子，口紅。

A In some countries, look people in the eyes when you talk to them.
在有些國家，與人交談時要看著他們的眼睛。

B It's my long time dream to be a backpacker.
我長久以來的夢想是成為一個背包客。

A The most important thing is safety.
最重要的是安全。

旅遊 4

1. This is my first visit to Moscow.
   這是我第一次到莫斯科。

2. What do you like best about Berlin?
   你最喜歡柏林的甚麼？

3. What is the Eiffel Tower famous for?
   艾菲爾鐵塔因何出名？

4. Look! There's a souvenir stand over there.
   看！那邊有一個紀念品攤。

5. Chewing gum is prohibited in Singapore.
   在新加坡禁止嚼口香糖。

禁止也可用banned、 forbidden、或not allowed。

旅遊 5

1. We have three holidays in a row.
   我們連續三天放假。

2. I m planning a visit to Kenting. Can I take Thursday and Friday off?
   我正打算前往墾丁。我可以週四和週五休假嗎？

3. When are you going on vacation?
   你什麼時候去度假？

4. Tomorrow is a national holiday. The zoo will be very crowded.
   明天是一個國定假日。動物園將會很擁擠。

5. What are your plans for Thanksgiving?
   感恩節你有什麼計劃？

6. I really need to get away for a week to relax myself.
   我真的需要遠離一個星期來放鬆自己。

寵物

A Please keep your eye on my puppy while I go to the restroom.
我去廁所時請你看著我的小狗。

B Ok, your puppy is so cute!
好，你的小狗好可愛！

A I bought it from a pet store.
答：我在寵物商店買的。

B I am an animal lover even though I'm not a pet owner.
即使我不擁有寵物，我也是個動物愛好者。

A Really? Do you join the animal rights group?
真的嗎？你有加入動物權利組織？

B Yes, we take care of homeless animals and find them suitable accommodations.
是的，我們照顧無家可歸的動物也幫它們找到合適的住宿。

寵物 2

A We need to clean the cage, it starts to smell.

我們需要清潔籠子，它開始有味道。

B What else should we do?

我們還應該做甚麼？

A We also need to change the water twice a week.

我們還需要一個星期換兩次水。

B I know that, do we need to brush her every day.

我知道，我們需要每天幫她刷毛嗎。

A I don't think so, just brush her once in a while. But I would love to walk her every day.

我不這麼認為，只要偶而刷一下。但我很想每天帶她去散步。

寵物 3

A Welcome to XYZ pet shop. What kind of animals you are considering?
歡迎來到 XYZ 寵物店。你們正在考慮什麼樣的動物？

B I prefer a dog but my wife is allergic to furry animals, so we want to get a pet fish.
我喜歡狗，但我的妻子對毛茸茸的動物過敏，所以我們希望養寵物魚。

Besides, we both work full time so we don't have time for training cats or dogs.
此外，我們都全職工作，所以我們沒有時間訓練貓或狗。

A You don't need to do nail trims and baths, either.
你們也不需要幫魚修剪指甲和洗澡。

B How often do we need to change the water?
我們多久需要換一次水？

寵物 4

Ⓐ What breed of dog are you interested in?
你對什麼品種的狗感興趣？

Ⓑ Golden retriever.
黃金獵犬。

Ⓐ What kind of dog do you have?
你的狗是哪一品種？

Ⓑ It's a mix.
它是一個混血狗。

說明

mix 是 "混合" 的意思。同理，mixed marriage 可指不同種族膚色的人通婚。

Ⓐ Wow! Your pet parrot is so beautiful!
哇！你的寵物鸚鵡是如此的美麗！

Ⓑ I also like its ability to mimic. That always makes me laugh.
我也很喜歡它的模仿能力。那總是讓我發笑。

飯店

1. The hotel is booked up for the Christmas holidays.
   聖誕假期該酒店房間已訂滿了。

2. Single rooms, double rooms, triple rooms and quad rooms.
   單人房，雙人房，三人房和四人房。

英文的唸法中，AA唸成double A，AAA唸成triple A。

3. All our rooms have free Wi Fi and a flat screen TV with 100 channels.
   我們所有的房間都有免費的無線網絡，液晶電視與100個頻道。

4. We have tea and coffee making facilities in every room.
   我們每間客房都有泡茶設施和咖啡機。

5. Our standard double rooms can accommodate up to four.
   我們的標準雙人房可容納到四個人。

飯店 2

A Do you have any vacancies tonight?
你們今晚有沒有空房？

B Would you like a smoking or a non-smoking room?
你抽不抽煙？

A Non-smoking. I will be staying for 2 nights. What's the room rate?
不抽煙。我將住2晚。房價多少？

B For a single room with a single bed, it's $60 per night plus tax.
一個單人房單人床，每晚60美元加稅。

說明

Single bed是單人床，Double bed是雙人床。一般說來，Queen size bed和King size bed也都是雙人床，但Queen size bed比Double bed大，而King size bed又比Queen size bed大。

飯店 3

1. I would like to make a booking for a single room.
   我想預定一個單人房。

說明

make a booking和 make a reservation都是預定，前者是英式用法，後者是美式用法。

2. What prices do your rooms start from?
   你們的房間從什麼價格開始起跳？

3. What day would you like to check in?
   你想什麼日子辦理入住？

4. When will you be checking out?
   你想什麼時候退房。

說明

check out除了當作 "離開飯店"，也可當作 "檢查"。例句：You must check out the whole system to make sure everything is fine. 你必須檢查整個系統已確保毫無問題。

飯店 4

1. During the peak holiday season, you had better make a reservation prior to arriving.
   在假日高峰季節，你最好到達之前要事先預約。

prior to 等於 before。

2. To secure the room, please pre-pay with a credit card.
   為了確保可訂到房間，請用信用卡預先支付。

動詞前面加 pre，表示"預先"。

3. Thank you so much for choosing our hotel, enjoy your stay!
   非常感謝你選擇我們的酒店，享受您的停留！

飯店 5

1. I have cancelled your reservation.
   我已經取消了你的預訂。

2. Do the rooms have internet access?
   房間能上網嗎？

3. Usually the youth hostels are more affordable for students.
   通常情況下，青年旅社讓學生更住的起。

4. We offer every room with handicapped facilities.
   每間客房我們都提供殘障設施。

5. In the public area, there's a kitchenette for you to prepare you own meals.
   在公共區域，有一間小廚房讓你為自己準備餐點。

6. Is there any porter to help me?
   是否有行李員可幫我？

飯店 6

1. To call the front desk, just dial 0.
   要打電話給櫃台，請撥0。

2. I am looking for a hotel with free parking and a nice view of the harbor.
   我在尋找一個酒店，有免費停車場，也可
   看到港口的美景。

3. Please bring us some more towels and
   amenities.
   請拿給我們一些浴巾和用品。

amenities是飯店免費提供的小用品，例如：
洗髮精、香皂、刮鬍刀等。

4. Welcome to Days Inn.
   歡迎來到戴斯酒店。

說明

Inn通常是較小型的飯店。

飯店 7

1. I need a guidebook to find a budget hotel.
   我需要一本指南，找到一家便宜酒店。

2. Do you have laundry service?
   你們有沒有洗衣服務？

3. Buffet style breakfast is served between 6 and 10.
   6點到10點間供應自助式早餐。

4. I will put the key card at the hotel counter.
   我會把鑰匙卡放在酒店櫃檯。

5. Our bell-boy will show you the room.
   飯店服務人員會帶你看房間。

6. We will provide you with a free sauna on your next visit.
   您下次來訪時，我們提供免費桑拿浴。

7. The honeymoon suite is on the 10th floor.
   蜜月套房位於10樓。

飯店 8

1. Hopefully I can spend a week alone at a hot springs resort.
   希望我能花一個星期獨自在一個溫泉會館度假。

2. How far in advance do they take reservations?
   他們多久前接受預訂？

3. Who can I ask for sightseeing advice?
   我可以向誰尋求觀光建議？

4. Some hotels give discounts if you stay during the weekdays instead of the weekends.
   有些酒店提供折扣，如果你在平日而不是週末假期入住。

weekdays是週間平日，週一到週五。
Weekends是週六和週日。

飯店 9

1. Our hotel gym is free to all patrons.
   You don't have to pay extra.
   我們酒店健身房免費提供服務給所有的顧
   客。你不必支付額外的費用。

2. Do you offer business services like
   printing and faxing?
   您們提供像列印資料和傳真等商務服務？

3. Can I make a toll-free call from my
   room?
   我可以從我的房間打免費電話嗎？

4. The lobbies are equipped with outlets
   so you can plug in your computer.
   大廳均設有插座，所以你可以將你的電腦
   插上。

5. The lobbies are also equipped with
   free wifi so you can log on when you
   need to.
   大廳還配備了免費 WiFi，這樣在你需要
   時就可以上網。

飯店 10

A Which one will give me a more deluxe vacation, a resort or a villa?
哪一個能給我更豪華的假期，渡假村或渡假別墅？

B It depends on how much privacy you desire.
這取決於你想擁有多少隱私。

說明

> resort和villa都是豪華的住宿套房，不同處主要在於resort所有房客享有共同的設施，而villa則是獨棟的，不共享設施。

A You may use the drinking fountain at the end of the hallway.
你可以使用走廊盡頭的飲水機。

說明

> frige是refrigerator的縮寫。
> hallway等於corridor。

飯店 11

A Hello, I am Dong Ming Lee in room 121. Is it possible to arrange a wake-up call for 6:00 am?

您好，我是121房的李東明，是否可安排上午6：00時叫我起床？

B OK, you'll get your wake-up call at 6:00 in the morning.

OK ，上午6：00時會叫你。

A I'd like to have some breakfast delivered to my room at 6.30.

6：30請將早餐送到我的房間。

B Sure. Would you also like me to arrange a taxi to the airport for you?

當然可以。你是否也要我安排一輛計程車去機場？

A That would be great. Can you order one for 7-30am?

這太好了。您可以訂在7：30嗎？

洗衣

A This is the hotel receptionist, how may I help you?

這是酒店接待員，請問有什麼可以為您服務？

B Do you offer laundry services?

你們提供洗衣服務嗎？

A Yes, we do. Do you need someone to pick up your laundry?

是的，我們有。您是否需要有人來收取你的衣服？

A Yes. Please send the laundry staff to my room now. My room number is 750.

是的，請洗衣工作人員來我的房間拿。房號是750。

B No problem, sir. Your clothes will be returned to your room before tomorrow evening.

沒問題，先生。明天傍晚前您的衣服就會送回。

轉交物品

A I'd like to leave a parcel for my friend. He will pick it up later. Is that okay?
我想寄放一個包裹給我的朋友。他稍後會來拿。行不行？

B By all means, just tell me your name, your room number, his name, and when he's coming by.
當然，只要告訴我你的名字，你的房間號，他的名字，他何時來。

A I will write it down for you.
我會寫下來給你。

B Thanks for your consideration! Is there anything else I can do for you?
謝謝你的體諒！還有什麼我能為你做的？

A That's all for now.
目前全部就這樣。

請人清理房間

A Reception Jennifer speaking. How can I help you today?
這是櫃台的珍妮佛，有什麼可以為您服務嗎？

B I'm staying in room 837. I would like you to send someone to clean the room.
我住在837房，我想請你派人來打掃房間。

A Do you want it now or later?
你想現在還是晚一點？

B Me and my wife are leaving in 15 minutes. Could you send someone after we have left?
我和我的太太 15 分鐘內將離開，離開後再派人。

A Is there anything else I may help you with?
另外有什麼可以為您服務嗎？

B No, that'll be all.
不，這就是全部。

MEMO

Chapter 11

健康

Health

健康

1. I hope you stay healthy all winter, there'll be no flu for you.
   我希望你整個冬天都保持健康，不會感冒。

2. Is it good for my health to slim down fast?
   快速瘦下來對我的健康好嗎？

3. After sleeping for 8 hours, I feel so fully charged.
   睡了八小時後，我覺得精力充滿。

說明

> fully charged 本來是指電池充滿電---The battery is fully charged. 但這裡是表示人充滿精力。

4. Tips to give you a sneeze-proof life.
   給你一個一生不再打噴嚏的訣竅。

Tips 是訣竅或提示。名詞後面加proof有"防止"的意思。例如：water-proof bag---防水袋。fireproof roof---防火屋頂。

健康 2

141

Ⓐ What is important to stay healthy?
保持健康最重要的是什麼？

Ⓑ Make sure you eat the right foods, do the right workouts.
確保你吃正確的食物，做正確的運動。

Ⓐ Tell me about your delicious meal plans.
跟我說說你們美味的膳食計劃。

Ⓑ They will help people fulfill their weight- loss goals.
那會幫助人們實現他們的減重目標。

Ⓐ Should I avoid foods high in calories or fat?
我應該避免高熱量或高脂肪的食物？

Ⓑ Certainly. But don't overdo dieting.
當然。但不要過分節食。

健康 3

A How much do you weigh?
你有多重？

B 70 kilos, about 150 pounds, I guess.
70公斤，約150磅，我猜。

A You're very fit.
你健康良好。

B I have started an exercise program to keep me in good physical condition.
我已經開始一個運動計劃，以保持我的身體狀況良好。

A Do you go hiking or bike riding or something like that?
你有健行或騎自行車之類的嗎？

B Actually, I run a marathon every week.
事實上，我每週跑一次馬拉松。

健康 4

Ⓐ How to eat right?
如何吃的正確？

Ⓑ Emphasize fresh fruits and vegetables. Protein and whole grains are also important.
強調新鮮水果和蔬菜。蛋白質和全穀也很重要。

Ⓐ What else should I do? Can you give me more tips?
還有哪些我該做？你能給我更多的秘訣？

Ⓑ You told me you never drink, right? There is one more thing: Don't overeat.
你告訴我你從不喝酒的，對不對？還有一件事：不要吃得過飽。

說明

over 是 "超過"。例如：Overdo--做的過多，Overdrink—喝的過多。

Ⓐ I can live with that!
那對我不成問題！

健康 5

1. Looks like you're in good health.
   看起來你是健康良好。

2. Take a nap after lunch. You'll feel more energetic in the afternoon.
   午飯後小睡片刻。你會在下午覺得更精力充沛。

3. Christy always warms up before working out.
   克里斯蒂運動之前一向先暖身。

4. A merry heart does good like a medicine.
   喜樂的心是良藥。

5. Laughter is the best medicine.
   笑是最好的藥。

6. Why fret about your situation? It's not gonna help.
   為什麼擔心你的情況？這不會有幫助。

健康 6

1. He yawned at lot when seeing this boring movie.
   他看這無聊的電影時打了許多個哈欠。

2. Taking a walk every day will do good to your lungs.
   每天散步對你的肺很好。

3. Give me a practical tip to kick this bad habit.
   給我一個實用的技巧來戒掉這個壞習慣。

戒掉壞習慣也可說 conquer a bad habit。

4. Ian dozed off during the class.
   伊恩上課時打瞌睡。

打瞌睡的另一個片語是 nod off。

健康 7

A You look so slim. I could hardly recognize you.
你看起來很苗條。我幾乎認不出你了。

B I've been on a diet for 3 months, and I'll keep on doing it!
我已經節食3個月了,我會繼續下去!

A You're not that fat. Don't make a big deal out of it.
你沒那麼胖。不要小題大做。

B I bought a running machine. Now I use it every day.
我買了一台跑步機。現在我每天使用它。

A You're really determined!
你真有決心!

B I am also attending a class called "maintaining a healthy lifestyle".
我也參加了一個課程,名為"維持健康的生活方式"。

減肥

A Wow! You look so skinny.
哇！你看起來很瘦。

B I lost 10 kilos in 2 months.
我2個月瘦了10公斤。

A You are really something!
你真了不起！

B This is what I do everyday: eat less and exercise more.
我每天少吃多運動。

A I wouldn't survive a day on a diet.
節食讓我無法生存。

B Come on! You are not overweight.
拜託！你沒超重。

睡眠

A It's time for bed. You need to get some rest.
睡覺時間到了。你需要好好休息一下。

B I'm not sleepy at all.
我一點也不睏。

A Try listening to some relaxing music, or drinking some hot milk.
嘗試聽一些讓人放鬆的音樂。或喝一些熱牛奶

B They won't work. Let alone I am allergic to milk.
這是行不通的。更別提我對牛奶過敏。

A Since when?
從什麼時候開始？

B Since birth.
從出生開始。

手術

Ⓐ What's wrong with your finger?
你的手指怎麼了？

Ⓑ I broke it yesterday playing tennis.
昨天打網球時弄斷了。

Ⓐ That's so terrible.
真糟糕

Ⓑ It really hurts.
真的很痛。

Ⓐ Are you afraid of having surgery?
你害怕手術嗎？

Ⓑ I've never had surgery before.
從來沒做過。

分娩

A Last time you told me your wife is 8 months pregnant.

Did she give birth yet？

上次你告訴我你的妻子有8個月的身孕。

她生了嗎？

B Yeah. I am a recent father of lovely twin boys.

是啊。我剛成為一對可愛雙胞胎男孩的父親。

A Congrats!

恭喜！

B Now I am pretty busy taking care of my wife and my babies.

現在我非常忙著照顧我的妻子和孩子。

A It's worth it!

這是值得的！

說明

congrats就是congratulations的縮寫。

生產

A Melinda gave birth to a girl last night.
梅琳達昨天夜裡生了一個女孩。

B It's good news. Thanks for telling me.
這是一個好消息。謝謝你告訴我。

A Her baby weighed 3.1 kg. She has her father's eyes.
她的孩子重3.1公斤，眼睛像她爸爸。

B Are you going to visit her and the baby?
你會去看望她和孩子？

A I have been expecting this day for a long time. Do you wanna join me?
我期待這一天很久了。你想和我一起去？

B Absolutely!
當然！

就醫

A How are you feeling?
你感覺怎麼樣？

B Not good.
不舒服

A What's bothering you?
是什麼在困擾你嗎？

B I got a headache.
頭痛

A When did it start to feel this way?
什麼時候開始有這種感覺？

B This Monday.
這星期一。

A I will prescribe medication for you.
我會開藥給你。

戒菸

A Hey Buddy. What's going on?
嘿，同伴。你在幹嘛？

B Taking a smoke break.
休息抽根菸。

A You ever tried to quit?
你有沒有嘗試戒菸呢？

B Many times. I'm really addicted. It's harder than you think.
很多次。我真的上癮。這比你想像的更難。

A Believe it or not. I already quit drinking. I will pray for you.
信不信由你。我已經戒酒。我會為你祈禱。

B Thanks. I'll talk to you later.
謝謝。待會再和你聊。

天氣

1. Summer is both hot and humid here in Taiwan.
   在台灣夏天既熱又潮濕。

2. It's really cold outside. You better put on a sweater.
   外面很冷。你最好穿上毛衣。

3. It's about 20°C or 68°F now in Taipei.
   現在台北約攝氏20度或華氏68度。

說明

F: Fahrenheit, 華氏。
C: Celsius, 攝氏。

4. What is the average temperature in Tokyo during November?
   東京十一月的平均氣溫是多少？

5. In some cities of the States, it's pretty chilly in the winter.
   在美國的一些城市，冬天很寒冷。

天氣 2

1. My favorite season of the year is autumn because it doesn't rain much.
   我一年中最喜歡的季節是秋天，因為它不會下很多雨。

2. The chance of rain today is 90%. Don't forget to bring your umbrella.
   今天下雨的機率為 90 %。別忘了帶你的雨傘。

3. The cool breeze in this season makes the weather pleasant.
   這個季節的涼風使天氣宜人。

4. Chicago is called the windy city.
   芝加哥被稱為多風的城市。

5. What's the indoor temperature?
   室內溫度是多少？

6. It's probably going to snow a lot tomorrow.
   明天可能要下很多雪了。

MEMO

_____

_____

_____

_____

_____

_____

_____

_____

_____

_____

_____

_____

_____

_____

_____

最多人使用的英語關鍵學習法

雅致風靡　典藏文化

親愛的顧客您好，感謝您購買這本書。即日起，填寫讀者回函卡寄回至本公司，我們每月將抽出一百名回函讀者，寄出精美禮物並享有生日當月購書優惠！想知道更多更即時的消息，歡迎加入"永續圖書粉絲團"您也可以選擇傳真、掃描或用本公司準備的免郵回函寄回，謝謝。

傳真電話：（02）8647-3660　　　電子信箱：yungjiuh@ms45.hinet.net

姓名：		性別：	□男　□女
出生日期：　　年　　月　　日		電話：	
學歷：		職業：	
E-mail：			
地址：□□□			
從何處購買此書：		購買金額：　　　　　元	

購買本書動機：□封面 □書名 □排版 □內容 □作者 □偶然衝動

你對本書的意見：
內容：□滿意□尚可□待改進　　編輯：□滿意□尚可□待改進
封面：□滿意□尚可□待改進　　定價：□滿意□尚可□待改進

其他建議：

總經銷：永續圖書有限公司

永續圖書線上購物網
www.foreverbooks.com.tw

您可以使用以下方式將回函寄回。

您的回覆，是我們進步的最大動力，謝謝。

① 使用本公司準備的免郵回函寄回。

② 傳真電話：（02）8647-3660

③ 掃描圖檔寄到電子信箱：

yungjiuh@ms45.hinet.net

沿此線對折後寄回，謝謝。

廣 告 回 信
基隆郵局登記證
基隆廣字第056號

2 2 1 - 0 3

 雅典文化事業有限公司　收

新北市汐止區大同路三段194號9樓之1

雅致風靡　典藏文化